BATTLE
BEYOND EARTH
RESURRECTION

NICK S.THOMAS

First published in the United Kingdom in 2014
by Swordworks Books.

ISBN 978-1-909149-67-0

Typeset by Swordworks Books
Printed and bound in the UK & US
A catalogue record of this book is available
from the British Library

Cover design by Swordworks Books
www.swordworks.co.uk

BATTLE BEYOND EARTH

RESURRECTION

NICK S.THOMAS

PROLOGUE

The year is 2512. Humanity first encountered intelligent alien life in 2134. All hope of coexistence with the alien race known as the Krycenaeans seemed lost, when they attacked Earth's Lunar colony and were quick to continue on to the Human homeworld. The prospect of defeat soon turned to a realisation that the Human race faced extinction.

Krycenaeans - a psychically powerful race; humanoid in form but with deep blue skin. Most stand half a metre taller than a Human, and further more when in armour. To the Humans of the 22nd century, the Krys were a ruthless and unrelenting foe that knew no fear and existed for no other reason than to fight and to vanquish other species. For them, Earth was a paradise worth sacrificing everything in order to conquer.

At first the brutality, superior technology, and countless assaults smashed humanity's armies. But many fought back in defiance with a hardened resolve and desperate will to live. Rapid advancements in technology and tactics allowed the armies of Earth to fight against the Krys Army, under their Lord Karadag, and eventually drive them from Earth.

But the Krys were soon to return in greater numbers, under the command of a far crueller and more formidable foe - Demiran, who would rather see the planet of Earth destroyed than leave it to humanity. But humanity found a hero, one who would eventually lead them to victory.

That is when everything changed. A third and final assault on Earth by the most powerful of the Krys Lords - Erdogan, left the armies of Earth devastated and defeated. In an act of desperation, a few million fled Earth in the hope of preserving the Human race. Pursued into a new system, all seemed lost, when the most unlikely of events occurred. Humanity discovered intelligent life once more, the Aranui, a race small in number, but technologically advanced beyond even the Krys.

With the help of new allies, humanity took back its homeworld and defeated Erdogan. The Allied victory brought a new age of peace and prosperity on Earth where three races now lived among one another. For hundreds of years the Solar System saw no sizeable wars. The almost apocalyptic wars of the 22nd century were an ever-distant memory, the heroes and battles long forgotten. Great fighters and leaders no longer revered; they had been relegated to history. An age of prosperity and peace seemed like it would never end, but nothing lasts forever.

CHAPTER ONE

"I've been waiting for this ever since I got charge of this ship. Seven years, and it's finally happening," Commodore Laska said quietly to himself.

He stood tall and proud at the forefront of the bridge of his ship, staring out at the jump gateway and watching the last few shuttles land aboard one of the frigates ahead of their position. The gateway was almost new, and fifteen times larger than the biggest vessel known to the four races. His dark blue uniform was closely cut to his body and displayed the gleaming silver chrome rank title on his right shoulder. Laska was of average height, but a strong and fit man, more so than most of the crew that was half his age. He was bald, but with a well cut trimmed beard and moustache. He could hear footsteps approaching and turned to see his XO approach.

"Final preparations are complete. We're just waiting on De Ruyter and Triglav, Sir," she said.

Laska nodded in appreciation. "Thank you, Commander."

Commander Breckinridge was a formidable woman, standing twenty centimetres over the Commodore's head, and always imposing to those under her command.

"This will all be yours one day soon," stated Laska.

"Sir?" she asked.

"I'm not getting any younger."

"You've got plenty of years left in the service yet, Sir."

Laska laughed.

"No need to keep buttering me up forever. I won't be retiring anytime soon, but I will surely be promoted to a desk somewhere before long. I worked my whole life to get a ship like this. A Monarch class vessel, and what a beauty she has been."

"UCN Bulwark is the finest that was ever built, and it has been an honour to serve aboard her," she replied.

Laska nodded in agreement.

He looked around the bridge and marvelled at the build quality of the vessel that was his home. It looked as new and clean as the day it was commissioned. Twelve of the crew sat at their consoles and awaited his command to take them through to uncharted space.

"Sir, I have confirmations from the De Ruyter and Triglav. Both are prepared for jump," stated Lieutenant Egland.

"Thank you, Lieutenant."

He looked back to the display screen once more. The five-metre high projection of space was displayed floor to ceiling and halfway around the walls of the oval bridge. The round space gateway was rotating now and beginning its start-up procedure. He took a deep breath and stepped over to his chair at the centre of the bridge, pressing a few keys on the console on one of the arms before turning back to the gateway. The crew fell silent on seeing the prompts projected before them that showed he was now live with the fleet of three vessels, including their own.

"This is the Commodore speaking. This mission has been many years in the making, but with the continued financial support of the United Colonies, and technical assistance of all those experts that have made this dream a reality, we are finally at that day. Kepler-186f is our destination, within the Kepler-186 system; a world that was discovered almost five hundred years ago, and yet remains unseen by Human eyes. Humanity has reached many worlds since we discovered space travel, but few have been habitable. Now the Aranui explorer is operational and ready for us to step foot there. Today we reach out to uncharted space and a world that could one day be rich with life. All crews prepare to jump, and remember this experience. It will be a great one that you should remember to the end of your days. Laska out."

He turned to Commander Breckinridge.

"Where is Santos?"

As he spoke, the Marine Captain strolled aboard the bridge and stopped in front of him.

"Captain, are your officers and drones at their stations?"

"Aye, aye, Sir."

"Are you expecting trouble?" Breckinridge asked.

"No, but I'd like to be ready for whatever possibilities we might face," Laska replied.

The Commodore looked past the Marine Captain to see a fully equipped combat officer standing at the entrance to the bridge. The mystery figure did not wear Marine pattern equipment, but that of the Army. He was in his early twenties and perfectly turned out, as if on parade.

"Who is that? I know everyone aboard this vessel, and I have not seen that man before."

The Commodore seemed as concerned as much as he was curious, and everyone knew there was a lot at stake. Santos was quick to answer.

"Sir, that is Second Lieutenant William Jones of the 2nd Airborne Regiment, out of the United Kingdom."

Jones stood a little above average height and had dark blonde hair. Everything about his appearance was carefully managed and organised, as to be nothing but the perfect presentation of an officer of an elite regiment. He was square jawed and despite his young age, had a look of confidence and experience about him.

Laska shook his head in amazement.

"One of his Majesty's paras aboard this vessel? How on earth did that come about, and why was I not informed?"

"I am sorry, Sir. The Sub-Lieutenant's appointment was last minute. I recently lost one of my best officers to the Haven Corporation, and this fine young man was quick to volunteer for the job."

"And is he up to the task?"

"I have every confidence in the fact, Sir. Second Lieutenant Jones came top of his class, has served with distinction and an exemplary career since his commission, and comes from a distinguished military family."

Laska groaned as he beckoned for Jones to come forward, and he did so promptly and with a salute.

"Well, Lieutenant, I can't say I'm happy with a last minute change to my crew, but welcome aboard, none the less. I assume the Captain here has brought you up to speed with our operating procedures?"

"Yes, Sir," he replied, "Sir, if I may speak?"

"We're about to make the most important journey of my career, so make it quick."

"Yes, Sir. I am very sorry for this rather unorthodox encroachment, but can assure you I will be nothing more than a valuable asset to your crew. I have no other agenda than to do my job, and serve my people as every generation of my family has done for as long as records exist."

"Sir, Jones' ancestor fought through the Krys wars, fighting in personal combat with the Krys Lords, Demiran and Erdogan."

Laska smiled.

"Well, well, that is some heritage, Lieutenant. Let's hope you can live up to your ancestor's great name and reputation."

"I will endeavour to do so, Sir."

The Commodore turned back to the view towards the gateway.

"Begin jump sequence!" he bellowed.

Lights flashed as the gateway fired into life. The structure was rotating at a great speed now, and the centre lit up until it was a swirling mass that appeared as if it would take them into oblivion.

"Jump gate activated and fleet prepared for jump," said Breckinridge.

Laska turned and looked around at the crew for one last time. They seemed as excited as they were terrified. None of them had ever made a jump into uncharted space before. It was a dream Laska had clung to as much as any of then, and yet the long wait had made their imaginations run wild with what they might find on the other side.

"Jump," stated Laska confidently.

He turned and watched the screen as their engines

drove them forward.

"Hundreds of years and we're still using these gateways. Maybe some day we'll have ships that can jump without gates," whispered Laska.

"If the Aranui will ever give up their technology," replied Breckinridge.

"They have their reasons."

"To withhold the greatest technology ever created?" she asked.

"If that technology had been available wholesale to the Krys during the wars, we wouldn't even still be around to tell the story. The Aranui know that the rest of us aren't ready for that."

"Will we ever be in their eyes?"

Laska shrugged. "Perhaps we will discover it when we are ready."

They both fell silent as they entered the swirling pool of energy suspended across the gateway and passed through. They had all gone through gateways more times than most of them could remember, but never to somewhere no Human had been before. The light from the energy inside the gateway was almost blinding until the ship's systems powered down the display screens for them to continue safely. There was nothing to see now as they waited, hoping and dreaming of what they might find the other side. Laska took in a deep breath, and as he began to breathe out, they suddenly emerged the other side, and the screens once again lit up. They found themselves marvelling at a small star, a little smaller and slimmer than the Sun far into the distance.

"Lieutenant Egland, confirm location."

She was quickly studying all the instruments before her

and then looked up.

"Confirmed, Sir. We have arrived at Kepler-186f."

The crew of the bridge erupted into cheers of excitement at the news. Laska marvelled at the star and several planets they could see on their screens. A map of the system displayed beside the image showed that they were close to 186f, but not currently on course.

"Take us around, set a course for 186f, and let's get a look at her with our own eyes."

The ship began to bank slowly to port, and everyone waited silently and with excitement to see the planet they had travelled so far for. They all knew Laska could have just as easily brought up the portside cameras on screen, but he'd rather savour the experience and wait till they were on course. The planet began to come into view, and not one of the bridge crew could find any words.

The world emitted a pinkish yellow colour from a largely canyon and desert-like surface, but they could already see areas of water even from the distance they were at. It looked like a hotter and drier version of Earth.

"It looks so much like Onesaka, Sir," said Breckinridge.

"You're right, but I'm not sure many of this crew have ever seen the Aranui world outside of pictures."

He reached down and opened a channel to the fleet.

"This is the Commodore. We have arrived at Kepler-186f, and our mission is to conduct a seventy-two hour research mission before returning to fleet HQ with our data. You all know what you have to do. Launch research shuttles, and let's make the most of the time we have. Providing the atmosphere is safe, we will commit Human resources to the surface within twenty-four hours. These are exciting times for all of us, but let's stay focused and all of us do our jobs. Launch when ready."

He turned back to the display screen to marvel at the world once again, just as most of the bridge crew were doing.

"Beautiful isn't it?"

"Outstanding," added Breckinridge.

But Santos and Jones looks entirely unimpressed, a fact that did not go unnoticed by the Commodore.

"You've travelled almost five hundred light years to a world no Human, maybe no intelligent life has ever been before. Is that not exciting to either of you?"

"Sir, until we have boots on the ground, and have an understanding of our environment, I will refrain from celebrating," replied Santos.

Laska smiled and was impressed at the professionalism while the rest of the crew were so blinded by the marvel before them, but he was also amused at how stern and serious the two of them were.

"And you, Lieutenant Jones? What does your gut tell you, now you can see this new world?"

"I would urge caution, Sir."

"Really? Enlighten me."

"Sir, it is better to be cautious and prepared than naive and headstrong."

"That is not the reputation of your Regiment," he replied jokingly.

"That reputation has long been relegated to history, Sir. We've moved past the stone ages."

Laska smiled once more.

"I assume then that you have already dispatched combat drones to the surface, along with the research teams?"

"Yes, Sir," replied Santos.

"And what kind of trouble do you expect to find on this uninhabited world?"

"I expect nothing, Sir, but I intend to be ready for anything."

Laska nodded in appreciation, as the first few shuttles came into view and increased speed as they soared towards the planet.

"What do you think you'll find down there, Sir?"

Laska shook his head.

"I have absolutely no idea, Captain, but I hope it is a new world for us to inhabit."

"Why, Sir?"

"Because we can, and that is Human nature. We will not stop exploring, expanding, and colonising anywhere that will sustain life."

"And maybe that will be our undoing some day."

"How do you mean?"

"Alien contact almost destroyed us once."

"Yes, and our second interaction led to our saviour, but I can see you're not too fond of non-Humans?"

Santos shrugged, and it was clear he was at least indifferent, if not hostile.

"I'm just glad this is an all Human operation for a change, Sir," he added.

It took two hours before the shuttles were finally getting through the atmosphere and heading for the surface, but not one of those on the bridge could take their eyes off the new world.

"First shuttle is preparing to land," said Egland, and they all watched from the camera feed on the front of the craft. The surface was dry and craggy with deep craters and tall canyons.

"Sir, drone three has identified an artificial construction."

Laska spun around in total amazement.

"What? What kind of construction? Get me an angle on that."

"Yes, Sir."

The screen changed to another feed, and they watched the shuttle soar over several canyons for over a minute. Then they caught sight of the anomaly. Three metal pylons stuck out of the ground and merged into one to form a perfect triangle, something that could only be manmade.

"Have the drone hold position to not approach any further," added Laska.

The camera feed stabilised as the shuttle came to a perfect hover, and they all stared at the object. It stood fifty metres tall.

"What on Earth is that?"

"Sir, I must insist that my combat drones investigate from here," added Santos.

"Yes, you do that," replied Laska without turning away from the sight.

Santos raised his arm and pressed a button on the console attached to the forearm of his uniform. A heads up display appeared before him showing a map of the area. He reached out and pressed an area of the artificial display.

"Alpha deploy here, Bravo here, deploy Falcon to two hundred metres here," he commanded, outlining the deployment.

"Give me eyes from those drones," ordered Laska.

The screens quickly split to show views from two drones from each squad and the aerial drone. The squads moved almost like Humans, but were entirely mechanical.

They were humanoid in size and shape, and even carried their rifles like a Human soldier would. The Commodore watched them disembark down a ramp onto the surface and begin closing in towards the target. He looked then to the Falcon aerial combat drone edging closer to the mysterious object. As it drew nearer, they could see on the surface beside the tower-like pylons a shallow dome fifty metres wide. It barely protruded above the surface and almost blended in seamlessly with the terrain, if it were not for its perfectly machined construction. It was coated in layers of dust and appeared as though abandoned.

"All units hold," ordered Santos.

Laska turned in surprise and waited for some explanation.

"Sir, we're still half a klick out, are you sure you want to investigate this?"

Laska was in utter shock and surprise, but soon he could not contain his excitement.

"Captain, we have waited years to get here, and upon arrival have found something none of us could have expected, something potentially life changing. We came here to explore, and I intend to do just that."

"And if this artefact presents a threat?"

"Then you have the means and skills to defend this fleet against any potential threats."

Santos was not convinced, but Laska wasn't ready to start throwing his rank around quite yet. He stayed calm and looked to Jones standing behind the Captain.

"Lieutenant?"

"Yes, Sir."

"New world, and a new discovery. What do you do? Investigate or leave it be?"

"Sir, it would not be my place to comment on operational matters. I am here to aid Captain Santos and act as an observer only."

"I'm still asking, Lieutenant, what do you think?"

Jones looked to Santos for permission, and the Captain was quick to give him the nod.

"Sir, I would investigate all potential areas of interest."

The Commodore smiled, but Jones continued, "However, when faced with the constructions of an advanced civilisation, I would recommend gathering data from afar and returning with greater strength. As the Captain says, I like to be ready and prepared for anything."

"Understood, Lieutenant, but we have one of the most powerful ships of the fleet and are more than a match for any potential threats. Captain Santos, proceed."

Santos grimaced for just a moment but went back to his display screens. He controlled the drone movements by hand gestures now on a projected display while the rest of the crew watched the screens. The drone was moving in a hundred metres ahead of the infantry.

"What do you think? Something abandoned from the Aranui?" Breckinridge asked.

Laska shook his head. "If they'd had any presence on this world, they would have told us when they assisted with the setting up of the gateway. I don't think any one of the four races has ever been here."

The pylon tower began to glow green at its base, and they could only stare in amazement as that energy began to rise up the length of the structure. It took just a few seconds for the energy to reach the peak, and then burst out towards the Falcon with such immense speed that nobody had time to react. The drone burst into flames, and the camera feed went blank. Many of the crew of the bridge gasped in horror.

Laska yelled, "Get our drones back!"

But it was too late. Alpha Squad was already in plain view as they made their way towards the tower, and bursts of energy hurtled towards them. Two of the drones were blown apart instantly, and the others took cover in the craggy landscape. Bravo had already gone to ground, and the tower could no longer find targets.

"Get them out of there now!" Laska ordered.

Santos was ordering Bravo back when they could see from one of Alpha's cameras that five objects were rising up from the surface of the dome. They were spherical and with a frame of engines around their centre. Some kind of canopy appeared as if it were part of the roof of the dome. They were each two metres wide and moved quickly towards Bravo as they made their retreat. Energy surged from these new fliers and strafed the drones and several were cut down.

"Alpha Squad, open…"

"Do not fire on them!" Laska interrupted the Captain, "We cannot risk an incident here!"

"We already have an incident here, Sir. There is an imminent threat before us, what are your orders?"

They turned back to the video feed. They were looking through the eyes of the leader of the squad who was looking out from the cover of a rocky outcrop and tracking a target with its rifle, waiting for confirmation to fire.

"Sir, Alpha Squad can't stay put, and they can't run. They have to fight. Do I have your permission to engage?"

They watched the drones duck down for cover as the ground around them ignited from the bursts of energy hurled at them.

"All right, do it!" Laska shouted.

"Alpha Squad, engage targets," Santos quickly ordered.

They watched the drone soldiers opened fire. They hit one of the targets with a burst of gunfire and seemingly caused it to change course, but had no other effect. Energy bolts crashed into their position, and the drones continued to return fire. A flash of light encompassed the display screen before it went black. They all knew what it meant, but Santos stated the fact anyway.

"Both squads are lost, Sir."

Silence overcame the bridge. Laska tried to come to terms with what they had seen, and everyone else looked to him for answers, but he remained frozen. Breckinridge broke the silence.

"Sir, I suggest we gather all data from here and leave before we find anymore trouble."

"Yes, yes. Okay, Commander, get it done."

He was still in shock.

"Sir, I'm getting interference on the scanners," stated Egland.

Laska seemed to snap out of his daze.

"What is it, Lieutenant?"

"Sir, I think a gateway is opening up."

"What? We're the only ones with access to this location."

"It's not our gateway, Sir."

"Put it on screen!"

They watched lights flash, and a gateway opened up before their very eyes. Eight metallic objects broke out of the swirling energy of the gateway. They formed a circle that was more than ten times as wide as the length of the Human vessel. They were evenly spaced and clearly from the same vessel and were slowly becoming more visible. They appeared to resemble a creature more than a machine, but the construction was artificial. The craft was just a ten klicks away from their position.

"Run scans on that thing. Tell me what it is and where it came from!" Laska ordered, "Have the De Ruyter and Triglav move half a klick forward of us. Put them in a flanking position between us and whatever that thing is," he added.

They watched the tentacle-like objects stretch further from the gateway, but then an egg-shaped metallic structure appeared at its centre. As the craft came further into view, they could see it was three times as long as its enormous width. The structure was a flat and dull black, and as the gateway's light began to fade, the ship appeared like a vast shadow in space. There were no lights of any kind on the structure, and only the light of the planet below formed the outline.

"What is that? Krys?" Breckinridge asked.

"No, I've never seen anything like it. It isn't one of the four races. Send out the first contact protocol, and begin an open channel on all frequencies. Let's try and see if we can get through to who or whatever this is," ordered Laska.

"I'm getting some kind of transmission, Sir," said Egland.

"Put it on screen."

The display went black. Laska looked back to the Lieutenant, but she had nothing to add. He turned to see a slight glimmer of movement in the darkness, and then two small red lights began to glow like eyes watching them.

"I am Commodore Laska of the United Colonies. We

come in peace."

The small lights grew brighter, but no response came. After a few minutes they could hear a faint hum that grew louder, almost like a growl.

"Sir, I'm getting a massive energy reading."

The transmission was cut off and returned their view to the hulking vessel. They could see energy pulsing at the centre of the ship, and it started a slow climb along the lengths of the eight pincer-like structures. It was just like the tower on the surface.

"Shields up!" Laska yelled.

"They saw a glimmer on the two friendly vessels before them as the shields activated. The energy reached the tips of the imposing ship, and they burst out to join one another, finally surging towards the De Ruyter. The shield flashed as it was struck, but appeared to offer little resistance to the immensely powerful energy that cut the frigate in half. Debris was scattered through space as the crew of the Bulwark watched in horror.

"Target that ship. Open fire with everything we've got! And begin jump gate sequence. Get us the hell out of here!"

The ship began to bank, but the view screens stayed fixed on the deadly vessel. Lights flashed as the weapon systems of the Bulwark opened up. Railgun shots and missiles impacted on the surface of the ship, and yet appeared to have no effect. A volley of smaller energy pulses flew from the craft towards the Triglav. The shielding absorbed the first few, but the three that followed smashed into the hull and tore holes in the structure as if not slowed by the armour at all.

The frigate was returning fire, but none of their

weapons appeared to be causing damage.

"We aren't gonna make it to the gateway! We can't take that kind of punishment!" yelled the XO.

"We could drop an EMP. It could be our only chance!" Santos yelled.

"They hit the EMP vessel, and we could be left floating dead out here," replied Breckinridge.

"And if we don't we're dead, anyway!"

"Do it!" Laska ordered.

Breckinridge rushed to a console nearby and put in her authorisation code. The others watched as the torpedo-like EMP vessel flew into view and rushed towards the alien craft. They could see the energy building at its core once again as it powered up its main weapon. They all knew that neither ship could survive its devastating effect.

"Twenty seconds until ignition! You know we're gonna lose shields when this goes off, Captain?"

"Not like they're any use right now, anyway," added Santos.

The countdown reached five seconds when the main weapon of the mysterious craft fired once again, and they watched in a terrified silence as the Triglav was blown apart. Just seconds later the EMP was triggered, and the guns of their ship stopped instantly, as did half of the screens and lights on the bridge, but they still had enough displays to see the enemy vessel had lost power.

"Status?" Laska asked Breckinridge.

"We've lost shields, targeting systems, life support on two levels, and a lot of auxiliary systems, but we still have engines."

"Then get us out of here, now!"

"Shouldn't we pick up survivors?" Jones asked.

Laska stopped for a moment. He was a little ashamed that the thought hadn't occurred to him, but even so he knew there was nothing they could do.

"We'll be lucky if we survive this, Lieutenant. Let's get out while we still can."

"Gateway sequence complete, Sir," said Egland.

"All power we have to the engines. Everything you can get."

They were closing the distance now, and many of the crew watched a small screen to their side showing the gateway they were heading for. The start up sequence was complete, and they were on course. But Laska still stared at the shadow of the alien vessel that had torn their small fleet apart. He looked at the ship as if expecting it to once again come to life, and Santos was close by doing the same.

"Sir, I've got something incoming from the target," said Egland.

They looked over the screens but could not make it out, but Egland brought up a camera that was tracking the unknown object. It looked like nothing more than a small tube that was tapered at either end, and only emitted the smallest of light from whatever propelled it through space.

"What is that? A weapon?"

"No idea, Sir. I am getting no readings of life aboard. Almost ten metres in length, and it is approaching us at speed."

"Can we reach the gateway before it intercepts us?"

"No, Sir."

"Have we got anything that can shoot it down?"

"We can't track something that small manually. There's nothing we can do," replied Breckinridge.

"Are they going for our engines?" Jones asked.

"Negative, Lieutenant. We're already on course for the gateway. Even if we lost all propulsion, we'd still make it through. There's nothing left for us to do but hope we can survive whatever damage that thing does. How long until impact?"

"Thirty seconds, Sir."

They watched the screen now as the mysterious alien object rapidly approached. They saw it come alongside, and it turned and plunged through the hull at the rear of the Bulwark, not far from the engines. It disappeared from view as if it had passed through thin air.

"We've got a hull breach on level three!"

The XO was already at the control screen and closing off sectors to ensure they maintained pressure. Everything fell silent while they waited for an explosion of some kind, but it never came.

"Get me a feed of whatever that thing is," said Laska.

The screen cut to a broad engineering corridor where the alien object rested peacefully on the ground. But before any of them could get a word out, they could see rods expand out from the object, and were soon joined by more. The device formed into what appeared like a ten-legged metallic spider. It stood almost two metres tall and quickly took flight. None of them could believe what they were seeing, but Santos was quick to leap into action.

"Enemy combatant aboard, all officers to their stations. Deploy Charlie and Delta squads to engineering."

"Sir, something is overriding our engines. Reverse and bow thrusters are firing. We're coming to a stop," said Egland.

"Well, stop them!"

"I can't. I've lost all control. Somebody must be accessing them directly from engineering."

"We're seconds away from escaping certain death. I won't be stopped by…whatever that thing is!"

"I can help," said Jones. He was the only person in the room in full armour and equipped to fight.

Laska nodded in agreement, and Santos was quick to put him to task.

"Get down to level three. Take drone squad Delta with you, and find that thing."

"And when I do?"

"Disable, kill it, I don't care. Just get rid of it!"

Jones nodded in approval and rushed out of the bridge with his rifle held at the ready.

"Delta Squad, on me at level three," he ordered over the comms.

He rushed down the ramps to the entrance to the third floor and found the squad of twelve drones were awaiting him.

"You two take point. Target is hostile. Orders are to kill or disable by any means necessary."

Two of the drones rushed onwards as he had ordered, and he took up position amongst them. It was a relief to have a shield of sorts around him, but he still had no clue what they were facing. They quickly reached the entrance to engineering and found three bodies scattered on the deck. One had been decapitated, the other two impaled by a large object. Jones knelt down to the two, but they were long gone.

Jones gestured to continue onwards, and they reached the main room of engineering to find two more bodies and an alien device connected to the centre console. It appeared to be a machine, and yet was pulsating like a living thing, like a parasite on the machine. Jones pointed for one of the drones to approach, but as they lay a hand on the device, they were struck by a surge of electricity. The blast was so large that it blew the arm off the drone, disabling it instantly.

The Lieutenant raised his rifle and fired a burst into the device until it went still and dropped off of the console, but they didn't have time to relax. They could hear the clatter of something thrashing through the storage containers up ahead and throwing them aside when the spider-like machine burst out in front of them. Jones fired, but the shots appeared to do little.

It rushed at Delta Squad as they fired back, smashing six of them to pieces with the sheer weight of its body and power of its legs. Jones took careful aim at what appeared to be a sensor array on its metallic body and fired a two-shot burst. These shots appeared to cause the creature some pain or damage, but it was still on its feet and turned its attention on him.

"Oh, come on!" he yelled in anger.

He leapt into a sprint to escape the creature and got to a blast door and slid through. One of the drones made it with him, and he hit the door locks. The creature smashed into the blast door with all of its force, and that even caused it to buckle slightly, but it held. Jones breathed a sigh of relief, but got up to see it race off in the opposite direction and on the route towards the bridge where he had come from.

"Captain, you've got incoming! We've destroyed whatever was taking control down here, but you've got big trouble coming your way!" he yelled into the comms.

He hit the door release and rushed on after the creature.

"What the hell are we supposed to do about that thing?" he asked, but he knew he wouldn't get a response from the drone at his back.

Jones rushed along the corridor, finding a number of bodies and wrecked drones along the way. At last he arrived at the bridge but was stopped dead by the devastation before him.

"What the hell!" he whispered to himself.

Most of the bridge crew lay dead, and blood was strewn across the deck where limbs had been severed. The huge mechanical creature stood at the centre of the bridge and held the Commodore up before it with one of its pincers driven through his shoulder. Jones could not even bring himself to move as he tried to find some way to proceed.

They were on emergency lighting, and sparks flew from exposed cables. He looked down; Santos was hurt. He was unable to get to his feet and was sitting against one of the consoles trying to reload his sidearm, presumably in some hopeless attempt to resist their attacker. Jones was frozen in the doorway as he stared as the carnage.

Snap out of it, he told himself.

He felt something tug on the slim exoskeleton of his armoured suit and looked down. Breckinridge was bleeding from a head wound and lying in Egland's arms. She was too terrified to move and simply sat crying.

"Are we moving?" Jones whispered.

Egland shook her head.

"What do you need?"

"Twenty seconds at that console," she said, pointing to the flight control deck behind the huge creature that still held Laska up as if it was inspecting him. Jones desperately tried to think of a solution. As far as he could tell the creature was on a search and destroy protocol, as well as determined to stop their ship from leaving.

He realised he only had one.

"You sure you can get us out of here if I give you enough time?" he asked Egland one last time.

She nodded. "Sure, you think I want to stay here to die?"

"I'll get this thing out of the room, then you do whatever you have to do. I don't want to be left out here any more than you do."

She wiped the tears from her face and nodded in agreement once again, as Santos managed to prime his pistol. He futilely fired a few badly aimed shots at the creature that could just as likely have hit the Commodore. It released its grip on Laska, drew its pincer from his shoulder as he cried out in pain, and rushed towards the Captain.

"Hey!" Jones hollered.

He raised his rifle and fired two short bursts into the monster. The higher calibre shots seemed to at least cause it to take note, even if they appeared to do no damage.

"You looking for me?"

The creature stopped for a moment and appeared to study him, recognising him from their previous encounter.

What have you done? he asked himself.

Without any more hesitation, the machine rushed towards him. He let go of his rifle, turned and ran. His suit boosted his speed, and he stormed down the corridor at a full sprint with the creature hot on his trail. He rushed for one of the life pods. It was all he could think to do. There was one up ahead at the t-junction at the end of the corridor. He looked back for just a second. The creature was closing on him, but he didn't slow down.

The opening to the lifeboat was an open broad access door, wide enough for three people to pass, and a forty-centimetre step to get through where the blast doors closed. He drew the only two grenades he had from his suit and continued on with all the speed he could get. At the last moment, he jumped into a roll and slammed into the base of the step. It brought him to a dead stop and knocked the wind out of him.

The creature fell over the top of him and through the access door, but he felt one of its razor sharp pincers cut into his left arm just below the shoulder. It had passed through his armour like it was going through butter. He looked up for just a second to see the creature had rolled a few metres into the lifeboat and finally come to a stop. He armed the grenades and tossed them in before reaching up for control panel. He lifted the safety casing and punched the launch button, just as the creature began to rush back towards him.

The blast doors sealed shut before him as he got to his feet and looked through the tiny window. The creature was just a metre away when the launch sequence started, and the boat was thrust out from the hull of the ship at immense speed. It was only fifty metres out when the grenades clearly blew because the engines cut out, and the vessel went into a tumble as it carried on. He saw no signs of the creature.

Jones breathed a sigh of relief, lifting his hand to activate comms.

"This is Jones. How long until we jump?"

The response came from Egland, "In five, four, three,

two, one…"

He felt the shift in gravity as they passed through the gateway and knew they were finally safe. He slumped back down against the blast doors and realised there was a pool of blood gathering beneath him. He reached around to find the source and instantly felt a soaring pain in his abdomen where he had been stabbed and not even felt the impact. He tried to get to his feet and call for a medic, but he couldn't carry on any further. He slowly lay down on the deck and hoped somebody would be coming for him.

CHAPTER TWO

Seventy-two hours later.

Lieutenant Jones awoke and quickly reached down for the wound he remembered in his abdomen, but only found scar tissue. For a moment, he was dazed and confused. He thought he was still on the floor where he had collapsed but looked around and discovered he was lying in a hospital bed, and only covered up to the waist. A female doctor was approaching.

"Where are we?"

"Welcome back, Lieutenant," the doctor replied in a calm and polite fashion, "You are aboard UCN Ares 4."

"Where we shipped out of?"

"That's right," she said, checking some readings on a display at the side of his bed.

"How long have I been here?"

"You arrived fifty-four hours ago."

"I can't have been unconscious that long?"

"Your injuries and blood loss were severe, Lieutenant. We could not operate on you without using EPR."

Jones looked confused. "Which is?"

"Emergency, Preservation, and Resuscitation."

"Oh, come on, suspended animation?"

She smiled and nodded slowly.

"You drained by blood and put me on ice?"

She laughed a little. "I assure you that EPR is a common and successful method of treatment for those patients who have suffered fatal physical injury."

He shook his head. "You know how many horror stories there are about it? Don't you ever watch the news?"

"I like to rely on facts and evidence, not mass hysteria, Lieutenant. You were going to die. We ensured your survival. I am sure your wife would not be bothered by a treatment that saved your life."

He groaned in approval, but then his mind returned to the events that led him to being so badly wounded.

"Did anything come through the gateway with us? How about the crew of the Bulwark? What about Commodore Laska? Did he make it?"

The doctor smiled in response, and it was clear to him that she wasn't going to give him any answers to his questions.

"You've been through a great trauma, Lieutenant. Your superiors have been notified of your condition, and somebody will be along for you shortly."

He sighed at the lack of a response he had achieved. Once again he looked down to the scar in his abdomen. The skin felt tight, and he knew something had happened, and yet he felt no pain at all, just a slight irritation.

"So that's it. I was at death's door, and now I just go back to work?"

She nodded in response. "You're all fixed up,

Lieutenant."

"And I don't have to do anything?"

"I'd try not getting impaled again," she replied with a smile.

He'd heard of such miraculous medical treatment, but he'd never seen it with his own eyes. Nobody he knew had served in a war or anything close to one, so injuries were nothing more than what they encountered in training.

"You know I've never so much as broken a bone?"

The doctor laughed. "Well you certainly have a story to tell now."

The doors to his room slid open, and two officers approached. One was a UCN Captain, the other an Army Intelligence officer of the UCA. He wore chrome Union flag dog collars and bore the rank of Major, but Jones had never seen either of them before. He could just make out two Navy guards at the door outside, both carrying sidearms.

"I'm in some kind of trouble, Sir?" he asked the Major.

The Major took his cap off and reached out his hand in friendship. Jones took it but was surprised at his informal approach.

"Good to see you awake and recovered, Lieutenant. I am Major Redford, and this is Captain Keegan. I am here to get to the bottom of what went on in Kepler-186. But before that can happen, I am here to escort you to an emergency conference where you will give your account first hand to military and civilian leaders of the four races."

Jones was speechless and could only stare at the Major, with his mouth hanging open and his eyes wide.

"I appreciate it's a lot to ask, and I know you have been badly injured, Lieutenant, but as I am sure you are well aware, your experiences and knowledge of an imminent threat to life are of vital important to us."

"How long have a I got?"

"No time at all," replied Redford and pointed to the fresh uniform hung behind Jones. He got up and pulled on the fatigues that he instantly recognised were his own. It was a deep, dark green uniform that was minimalist and well cut to his body. His rank was displayed in chrome on his right shoulder, and his name printed in the sky blue text of his Regiment on his left chest. He pulled the shirt over his head, and it fitted like a glove. There were no buttons at all, but the collar rose high with a clasp that he fixed. He slipped into his black shoes and rolled his sleeves up into short sleeve order. Lastly, he took his maroon beret from the rack above the hanger. It was antiquated and a treasured item that was a symbol of his elite heritage.

"Can't believe you're still wearing those things," joked the doctor.

Jones smiled. "You have to earn this," he replied with a smile.

He nodded to Redford to say he was ready, and they led him out of the room. The two armed guards waited for the three of them to pass before continuing on at their rear.

"I'm not a threat, you know?"

"We know that, just like we know there is no fifth race alive today, or alien life in the Kepler-186 System. What we think we know might just have been blown out of the sky. I hope you can answer some of the many questions we have. Until that time, you will understand if we are a little cautious of everything that came back with you?"

"Yes, Sir."

He was led to an elevator and taken up several levels to a conference room where they found six bodyguards waiting. Only two of them were Human. Two were Krys, the hulking and strong adversaries who had once tried to hard to conquer Earth. They stood half a metre taller than the tallest Humans and wore ornately decorated armour. It was hard to not be intimidated by their presence, and the two-metre long poles they carried for self-defence that were both projectile and close quarter weapons; the only skin on show on their heads where their helmets were folded back. Their skin was a dark blue. Each of them looked as strong as an ox.

"There are Cholan representatives here as well?" Jones asked, surprised.

"Of course, the four races, as I said."

"We know a people for a few years and we're all buddy, buddy? How do you know we can trust them with this?"

"It's been almost fifteen years, Lieutenant. They have just as much right to be here as anyone. They have shown nothing but friendship and cooperation towards us."

The Cholans averaged just one and a half metres tall, more than a head height shorter than even the average Human. Their bodies appeared weak and fragile. They were humanoid in shape, but their shoulders were barely any wider than their heads, and their arms dropped down to their knees, more like an ape than a Human. They were an intelligent race, but Jones like many Humans, were still suspicious of their arrival and niceties.

"Don't cause an incident, Lieutenant. You're here just to help us understand what you experienced," said the Major.

"Don't worry. I wouldn't pick a fight here. It would be a

choice between fighting a child or a giant," he joked.

Redford stood up beside the eye scanner next to the doors. They soon slid open, and Jones was led inside. A Krys Lord was there to greet him. He had never met the alien before, but he knew his face and his attire well enough.

"Lord Jafar," he said in surprise, "It is an honour to finally meet you."

Redford looked surprised at how he had gone from such hostility to an alien to such respect, and Jafar was equally surprised.

"You served with my ancestor. Captain Charlie Jones of the 2nd Inter-Allied Regiment, one of the Immortals who fought with you and Colonel Mitch Taylor."

Jafar nodded in agreement. He moved like an old distinguished King and wore the highly decorated armour to match. Blackened armour with gold and silver inscriptions on every surface so that it almost appeared as some form of bizarre camouflage pattern. His face was paler than any Krys he had ever met.

"Great days, and a very long time ago," said Jafar.

"I'd love a few moments of your time to talk about my relative."

"Jones was a great man, one who wanted to have me dead more than a few times. I wish I could tell you more, but there are pressing matters at hand. The past can wait."

Jones could not believe his eyes. He was before one of the main leaders of the Krys people without any warning. An alien he had dreamed of meeting and talking with for as long as he could remember. But the history he had been brought up on was of no interest to those in the room. Redford ushered him forward to take a seat amongst a semi-circular table. Twenty-one sat at the table, all facing inwards, and more than fifty screens lay before them with other representatives of the four races. President Isaacs was at their centre, an American and the current leader of the Alliance. Jones had only ever seen him on television.

Isaacs was a Chinese American, a short, but fit man for his advancing years. He always looked so friendly and approachable on the news, but not anymore. He looked ready to put Jones in the ground.

"Lieutenant Jones, I believe?" Isaacs asked.

"Yes, Sir," he replied, though he wasn't sure of the protocol for talking to the President of the Alliance.

"Glad you could join us. Over the past forty-eight hours we have been trying to piece together what happened in this far away system, Kepler-186. So far, we have heard from a few members of the crew, but those who survived experienced very little that could assist us. You, on the other hand, were conscious throughout and engaged with this Unidentified Object first hand. You know how long it's been since we encountered a UO that could not be explained in forty-eight hours, Lieutenant?"

"Probably first contact with the Cholan, Sir?"

He shook his head in amazement. "We knew who they were within twelve hours of contact. They made themselves clear from the beginning, and neither of us fired a shot in anger. So I want you to explain to me how this potential first contact situation ended in such disaster? We could have a war on our hands, Lieutenant, and I want to know why."

Jones turned from humbled and confused to defensive.

"Sir, Commodore Laska did everything in his power to approach whatever it was we found out there in a peaceful fashion. Not once did we present a threat, and never did we engage a target until we had ourselves been fired upon. We defended ourselves when we had no choice, and I will not apologise for that."

The President looked shocked, but it was Jafar who intervened.

"Lieutenant Jones," he stated.

All attention turned to the Krys Lord.

"The Bulwark's systems were heavily damaged during the events in Kepler-186, and most of the video recordings via the drones were destroyed also. The footage recorded by the feed on your armour is one of the only sources of information we have on what attacked the Bulwark. It has taken your technical experts almost this long to restore the footage from your damaged camera, can you explain to us what it was that attacked you?"

Jones was like a rabbit in a spotlight until Redford stepped forward and started a video.

"This is all that we managed to recover from the camera on your suit, Lieutenant. The camera was destroyed, and the data storage was damaged also, but this is what we have."

The video began with his first encounter with the spider-like creature, though the footage was grainy and skipped many frames like some badly preserved film that was hundreds of years old. Even the colours faded in and out. There were just twenty seconds of footage, all involving his battle with the terrifying creature.

"This it? What about before when we engaged the enemy vessel and what happened on the surface of the planet?"

Redford shook his head. "This is all that has survived.

We have already heard statements from Commodore Laska and a handful of the crew who made it, but their recollection of events is varied at best."

Jones watched the video feed once again and noticed the feed cut off after he rolled into the step in front of the lifeboat, leaving out any evidence of how he was injured and rid them of the creature.

"One of the lifeboats was jettisoned. Lieutenant Egland believes the creature seen in your video recordings was aboard that boat, is that correct?" Redford asked.

"Damn right, Sir."

"That was the only physical evidence of what attacked your fleet, and you saw fit to return home without it?"

Jones couldn't believe what he was hearing.

"That *thing* tore our ship apart. It killed god knows how many crew, and our weapons were useless against it. If I hadn't got it off the ship, we wouldn't be here to tell the tale!" he replied in defence.

"We understand your standpoint, Lieutenant," replied President Isaacs, "But we lost two ships out there. The Bulwark is in need of months of repairs and refits, and we have lost the lives of four hundred and ninety-one souls. I hope you can understand that we need some more concrete answers."

"I'll give you an answer, Sir. Whatever it was out there, it was big, bigger than any warship I've ever seen. It was immensely powerful, and it wanted us dead. You want my advice? Gather the most powerful ships of the Allied races, go back to Kepler, and blow that thing to hell before it comes here to finish the job it started."

"We are considering all possibilities," the President replied calmly, "Have you got anything more to add?

Anything that might help us understand this disaster and deal with it?"

"Just kill this while we have the chance, Sir."

"Thank you, Lieutenant, you are dismissed."

He turned to leave as the delegates behind him launched into discussion, but Jafar stepped out to talk with him at the edge of the room. He was more than happy to hear anything the alien had to say. He was still suspicious of the Cholans, but there were none he would trust more in the Universe than Jafar. He had grown up on the legends of the alien's battles alongside his ancestor and Taylor, the hero of Earth, a man who seemed all but forgotten now.

"I cannot talk right now, Lieutenant, but I can spare you a few moments when this meeting is over. Meet me in Zenobia's Garden at 1900 hours, and we will talk further."

On any other day Jones would have been delighted with an audience with the alien Lord, but he was overwhelmed by everything that was being thrown at him. A nod of agreement was all that he could manage before the alien turned back to the other delegates. Jones had trained and worked beside the Krys before, but Jafar was more imposing than any of them. It wasn't just his elaborately detailed ceremonial armour, and he didn't even appear to carry any kind of weapon. It was his height, his presence. He looked and moved like a veteran of the ages, and Jones knew that was exactly what he was.

Jones shook his head in amazement that he had finally got to meet the great Jafar, the first alien ally of the Human race. He turned to leave and was met by the best sight he could have expected. A beautiful woman stood before him in her Navy flight officer's uniform. Her black hair was tied up and out of the way, and she appeared close to tears upon sight of him. It was his wife, Cynara. She rushed into his arms and held him tight before pulling back to look into his eyes.

"Are you okay? They said you almost died?" she said, tears now pouring down her face.

He smiled as he reached up and wiped the tears from her face.

"Do I look almost dead?"

She shook her head, and he turned and led her away towards his quarters aboard the station. But as she held him close as they walked together, all he could think about was his experience at Kepler. A hundred questions were rolling around his head, and he just prayed Jafar would have some answers for him.

He stepped into his quarters and slumped down onto a small hard sofa in what was more a cupboard than a room. The sofa was also a bed, and a tiny washbasin, shower, and wardrobe lay opposite. Almost every part of the little room was a shade of grey, and there was no decoration of any kind.

"Are these the quarters they gave you?"

"I'm lucky to have gotten this much. You know what premium there is on quarters on Ares 4? I'm surprised I wasn't tossed in with the ORs."

"So when are you coming home?" she asked, sitting down beside him.

He looked confused. "What do you mean?"

"You came out here to serve aboard the Bulwark. She's a wreck right now, and you just barely survived the experience. There's nothing left for you here."

"You're wrong. I have worked all my life to get here. I want to be there when we make history. I want to be a

43

pioneer and a part of something great."

She shook her head in disbelief.

"This is about your family again."

He didn't deny it.

"I know you come from a proud family with a lot of history, but dying in the service of the colonies is not doing service to that name."

"Then what, my ancestors who fought and died for us to be here today, that meant nothing?"

"You know that's not what I meant," she quickly snapped back.

He opened his mouth to speak but realised he was heading for a fight he didn't want or need.

"Let's just see where this takes us okay?" he asked.

She nodded in agreement.

"You really think it is a new race you found?"

"Has to be."

"Meeting the Cholans was one of the best things that ever happened in our lifetimes. Maybe there is hope for peace yet? Who knows what we could learn from such an advanced race?"

Jones stayed silent.

"We can't just accept that this is war," she continued, "We've never known war, and neither did our parents or theirs. The Human race was almost made extinct to win the peace we enjoy today. Are you ready to throw that away so quickly?"

Jones could no longer hold his tongue. He was getting more and more angry as she went on.

"You think I want war? Not that it even matters. If this new race wants war, then it's war. We can't ask them nicely to stop and just all get along. They fired the first shots, and they weren't fired as a warning. They hit hard, and they didn't stop."

"But we don't know that yet. This was one incident. It could be isolated. They could have just felt threatened. I hear some kind of machines attacked you. Maybe it was a programmed response or defence mechanism."

"Where did you hear that?"

"Rumours are rife through the fleet, Will. It's all anyone has talked about these last two days."

"And what do those rumours say?"

"All kinds of things, so nobody really knows what is going on. All we know for sure is the fleet you went out on came back in pieces, and with a lot of dead and wounded. A lot of people are asking a lot of questions and not getting any answers from the fleet. People are getting pretty anxious."

"Anxious? Well, yeah, they should be. We've got big trouble coming our way."

"I wish you would just tell me more about what happened out there. I can't stand being in the dark."

Dark? he thought.

It cast his memory back to the ominous eyes they had seen on screen when the alien vessel made contact with them. It sent a shiver down his spine to think of what kind of monster he was looking at. His imagination was going wild with what sinister or terrifying beast they were dealing with. Cynara could see the horror in his eyes now, and her tone changed completely.

"Maybe you should get some rest?" she asked sympathetically.

It broke Jones out of his dream-like state, but it took him a moment to be fully aware of his surroundings and take in what she had said.

"No...no," he said quietly, "I've been sleeping for two days. Right now, I need information."

He looked at the console on the wall to check the time and sighed impatiently, knowing he should leave for his meeting with Jafar.

"You really should rest, nonetheless," added Cynara.

But he jumped to his feet.

"No, I've got to get to a meeting."

"So soon? I just got here?" she pleaded.

"And I am glad you came. But there is work to be done. We'll talk soon."

With that, he stepped out and strode on at speed. Cynara looked unimpressed, but she knew he would not be stopped. Jones headed for the Garden where Jafar had agreed to meet him. He'd heard of Zenobia's Garden but never visited. It was one of a handful of artificial gardens on board the vast station built as places of tranquillity for people to relax, especially those still strongly attached to their homes on Earth. He had never felt such an appeal to fresh air and dirt, and didn't find the time or necessity to visit the artificial gardens either.

It was a fifteen-minute walk, and he passed hundreds of military personnel and civilians en route. He had almost reached his destination when a news anchor stepped out in front and blocked his way. A soccer ball shaped drone floated at head height beside the woman with the name of her company. She was smartly dressed in a single piece business suit, and her hair up and fixed so perfectly it looked false. A smile stretched across her face as she approached, but it was so fake it was almost funny.

"Lieutenant Jones? I am Winona Walters, UCNN. Can

I have just a few moments of your time?"

"Sorry, Miss Walters, but I am on duty and at work," he replied and side stepped, trying to get past her. But she moved over, and her drone camera blocked his path.

"You were aboard the Bulwark on her mission to Kepler-186, were you not?"

Jones sighed.

"I'm not at liberty to divulge operational information, Ma'am."

"But you were aboard the ship, weren't you? Can you provide some explanation as to the critical damage of the vessel, and the fact that you returned without the Bulwark's two support vessels?"

"No I cannot."

He stepped forward, shoved the drone out of the way, and carried on. The reporter sighed as if to be offended by his actions, but he could not help but feel he was the offended party. Then the sign was before him, 'Zenobia's Garden.' There was an open archway into the garden, and it was a bizarre sight to see green grass and trees just centimetres away from the steel floors of the station. He stepped inside and instantly noticed how great it smelt. The trees looked real, and he looked up at the sky and sunshine glinting across the tops of the trees fifty metres high. He knew it was artificial, and that much of what was above and in the distance was projected, but it was so effective he found his mind telling him it was real.

He carried on down a smooth path that led into the park to hear the sounds of birds and squirrels running about the scenery. It was similar to a luscious park he had visited in England when he was younger, and later during training. He was entirely immersed in the fake world when he heard his name being called and found Jafar standing in front of him. His two bodyguards stood off in the distance, ensuring they were left in peace.

"Lord Jafar, thank you for seeing me."

"What can I do for you?"

Jones took a deep breath and tried to think. He'd wanted to meet Jafar for so long and discuss his family's history, but now his mind couldn't leave recent events.

"I am sorry, but I am speechless. I just can't stop thinking about Kepler."

Jafar nodded slowly.

"Yes, it is a worrying situation. More so than you realise, I think."

"How can you know that?"

Jafar pointed to his flank, and he turned to see Irala with them as if he had just appeared out of thin air.

"What's going on here?" Jones asked.

He felt uneasy and couldn't understand how two such powerful leaders would come to him. Irala looked expressionless and statue like. He was taller than a Human but of much slighter build. But he had presence, and the look of a highly knowledgeable and advanced being.

"Why are you here?" he asked again.

"Lieutenant, during the conference with the Allied leaders, we were honest, though we did not disclose all that we know."

"Why? And why are you telling me?"

"Does the name Bolormaa mean anything to you?" Irala asked.

"No, should it?"

"I would hope not."

"What has this got to do with anything?"

"Bolormaa is a name that would strike fear into the heart of any creature, should they know who she is, or was. Bolormaa is a legend among my people. She led her armies throughout the galaxy, destroying all that stood before her."

Jones' interest in history sparked is imagination, and he let himself be reeled in.

"When was this?"

"Thousands of years ago. Long before I entered this life, but all of my people know of the Scourge of Bolormaa."

"The Krys are largely ignorant of this history now, but if you delve deep enough into our history, you will find it," added Jafar.

"Bolormaa led her people, the Morohta, in a devastating sweep throughout the galaxy. Several races were utterly obliterated by her armies, and the rest of us barely managed to survive. Many great battles were fought, but she could not be beaten," said Irala.

"So what happened?"

"That is the greatest mystery of our existence, and the question we all seek the answer to, though have been too terrified of what we might one day discover."

"And how is this relevant now? Why is this so important that you would both come to me?"

Irala held out his hand, and a projection appeared before him. It was the video from the Lieutenant's camera when he fought the robotic creature about the Bulwark. It made him sick to see it for a second time in the same day.

"That thing, the object that tried to kill you, and the ship you were aboard. We have seen this before."

Irala pointed to the projection screen that changed to a

dark interior room with what looked a lot like the creature, but frozen as if in a photograph, and yet it was a video panning around the object as two Aranui experts were analysing it.

"This is an artefact that has been in our possession for a very long time, and which is documented as having come from the time of the Scourge," said Irala.

Jones paced closer to the projection to study it more carefully. It was not an exact match to what he saw. It looked a little smaller, with more spindly legs and a shorter body. But it still bore a remarkable resemblance to what he was attacked by. It certainly looked very similar.

"You think this is the same origin?"

Jafar nodded.

"Why didn't you tell the Council?"

"Because we do not know for certain," Jafar answered, "And if this is true, it could spark chaos amongst the Allied nations."

"This Scourge, how were they stopped?"

"They were not stopped," replied Irala.

"What do you mean? You beat them, right? Or you wouldn't be here."

"No. Bolormaa destroyed fleets and armies one after another. Our people fought back for as long as they could, as did others. But we could not win. Then the fighting stopped. The Morohta fleets withdrew and vanished."

"Just like that? They took you to almost complete destruction and simply stopped?"

Irala nodded.

"And neither of you has any idea why?"

"It is the great unanswered question of our history. Almost so far back that it has been forgotten."

"There is barely one among my kind who even knows the story of Bolormaa any longer," Jafar said.

Jones was trying to take in all that he was being told. He suddenly felt very small in the world, despite being pushed to the forefront of events.

"Why are you telling me? You can't put this on me. It's too important. You can't put this on me!"

"Lieutenant Jones."

He turned and was fixated on the alien Lord.

"I knew your ancestor well. He was a great man, a great fighter, and a great leader. I know that blood flows through your veins, and we need the man that you were born to be."

CHAPTER THREE

"Lieutenant Jones reporting for duty, Sir."

It was déjà vu, and not the good kind. He was once again stepping onto the bridge of a vessel that was embarking for Kepler-186. It was another Monarch class and was hard to tell apart from the Bulwark, a class of vessels that had always felt like dreadnoughts to Jones until he went to battle in one. The Captain turned to welcome him. She was in her early forties and matched his height. She had light blond hair and a pale complexion, so much so that she appeared Scandinavian, but then she opened her mouth.

"Welcome aboard the Guam, Lieutenant. I am Commander Cohen."

Jones was surprised to hear her speak with a thick South American accent.

"Good to see you're along for the ride."

Jones turned to see Santos off to his side.

"You're not the only one who got patched up," he added.

Jones was glad to see a familiar face, and the Captain

reached out his hand in friendship. As he took it, Santos pulled him in close to whisper into his ear.

"I'm not in any doubt as to how we got out of there alive and who pulled it off. I'll not forget it."

Jones nodded in appreciation as Cohen continued.

"As combat leaders with firsthand experience, you are here not just as advisors. Lieutenant, none of us knew what you might find out at Kepler. Most thought you'd find nothing at all, but we were wrong. You weren't prepared for a fight the first time around. That will not be allowed to happen a second time."

She stepped aside and pointed to the screen projected beside her, and Jones looked out to marvel at the fleet, fifteen Human ships, including two more Monarch class vessels. Five Krys vessels, two of which dwarfed their capitol ships, a single Aranui vessel, and three Cholan.

"Impressive," replied Jones.

But he didn't believe the words he was saying. Before his experience in Kepler, he would have thought their fleet was enough to overcome anything, but now he was not so sure.

"Lieutenant, I am giving you command of Charlie Company. Now this may sound very irregular, but you have to remember that our Marine officers have training for this, but they have not seen action. You proved your worth aboard the Bulwark, and I'd like you to do the same for us."

"Yes, Sir."

"The fleet is assembled, Commander. We are all squared away and ready to jump," said the XO.

"Thank you, Captain Nichols."

Jones looked around at all the crew aboard the bridge.

They were mostly fresh faced and not long out of the Academy, just like he was. But unlike him, they appeared ignorant of the danger they were about to face.

"Open a channel to the fleet."

The XO nodded to confirm she was live.

"This is the Commander speaking. We are about to begin our journey to Kepler-186, a system that was previously thought to be uninhabited. The Bulwark found that to be untrue and paid a heavy price. We shall not make that mistake. We have assembled the greatest fleet seen in my lifetime. We are prepared. We know the dangers we face, and we have the resources and ability to deal with whatever and whoever may be out there. Whatever it was that struck the Bulwark, we do not know its origins or full strength. If we have to fight, then we'll sure put up a good one. But if this can be resolved peacefully, it will be. Nobody fires on a ship, nobody opens gun ports, or threatens anything we might find there, without my express permission. Let's not pick a fight, but be ready to end one if that time comes. That'll be all, prepare to jump. Cohen out."

The gateway was now active, and the fleet soared forward.

"You look scared," Cohen said to Jones.

"Yes, and you would be, too, if you had seen what we saw," Santos replied for him.

"Whatever is out there, you don't have to fear it any longer. We go in right this time," she replied.

Jones was still not convinced.

They passed into the gateway, and Jones could feel his stomach churn as he thought of the prospect of seeing the vast alien vessel once again. There was none of the excitement he felt the first time. He was asking himself why he was crazy enough to volunteer, but it was too late now. They passed through the gateway into the light of Kepler-186. The first thing they saw was part of the hull of one of the Bulwark's support vessels still floating in space and with debris all around it. Other than the remnants of the battle, the space was completely peaceful.

"Scan the area with everything we have. I want to know if we're alone out here. And set a course for 186f," ordered Cohen.

Once again Jones watched as they banked, and the planet came into view. But there was no excitement this time. There was no hope; only a fear of what was coming next. He could feel sweat dripping down his face now, despite the fact the ship's temperature was carefully monitored and regulated. Cohen noticed his perspiration and smiled sympathetically.

"Don't worry so much, Lieutenant. We're here to end this threat."

As the Commander's words came out, a flash of light erupted on screen and soared towards them, striking just as she turned to see the impact. They were thrown violently off their feet, and the lighting fluctuated for a moment. Cohen pulled herself up onto her chair and barked her orders.

"Shields up! Prepare to launch fighters!"

She looked over to the XO for a report.

"Minor hull damage, but we're okay," replied Nichols with a sigh of relief.

"What the hell was that?" Cohen yelled.

"I'm getting nothing on the scanners, except for...a small energy signature two klicks ahead."

They looked back at the screen to see nothing but space

between them and the planet. But before they could do anything, the lone Aranui vessel opened fire. Its beam-like weapon soared out to what seemed like open space until it appeared to pierce an object. A moment later the target seemed to materialise, as if from some camouflage device, and break apart from the high-energy blast.

Nobody said a word as all watched and waited for what would happen next and carefully studied the wreckage of the ship that had just been destroyed. It was smaller than a Human frigate. It had what appeared to be three talons or mandibles protruding from an oval and almost featureless hull, though it was hard to tell for sure, as the powerful blast had ripped the vessel apart.

"Is that the ship that attacked the Bulwark?" Cohen asked.

Jones shook his head.

"If only," he replied.

As he finished, a flash of lights burst out in the distance, and a volley of gunfire soared towards them as three similar vessels revealed themselves.

"Brace for impact!" Cohen ordered.

Just one of the shots hit the Guam, and it rocked them once again. Warning lights flashed over the console where the XO was already sectioning off floors that had been breached.

"Launch fighters and fire everything!"

The railguns opened fire and were quickly joined with trails of missiles as the crew did exactly as ordered. Another impact struck the Guam, and somehow Jones couldn't believe they were still alive. Off to their flank they could see a flash, as one of the smaller Human frigates was blown apart and another Cholan vessel was smashed so badly it lost power and was now nothing more than a floating wreck.

The Allied fleet did not need any direction to return fire. They joined the Aranui vessel and the Guam in unloading a salvo into the hostile vessels.

"The Manchester has been destroyed!" Nichols called out.

But their attention remained focused on the enemy vessels. They watched as waves of fighters swooped in to attack. Jones couldn't help but feel helpless as he watched everyone around him fight the battle while he did nothing but stand and watch and hope for the best.

The fighter wings strafed one of the enemy vessels, and the continued bombardment from the rest of the fleet smashed them into oblivion. Even as one of the wrecks began to break apart, the guns of the Guam continued pounding into its hull just to be sure.

"Hold fire!"

"All vessels hold fire," Nichols relayed the order.

Everything fell silent, and the bridge crew stared out into space at the wreckage of the alien vessels. On the side screens they saw the devastation to their own fleet. Everyone was frozen now, but Commander Cohen was checking the displays at Nichols' console. She seemed to keep going through anything with a cool head and professional touch.

"Leave three ships here to carry out rescue and research operations. Set a course for 186f, and get us moving," she ordered calmly.

No one moved for a second as they took in the horror of their own losses.

"You can save lives and protect even more if you get to

your jobs, so get to it!" she barked.

The engines drove them forwards once again. Jones approached the Commander with Santos close behind him.

"What exactly is our mission here, Sir?" Jones asked her quietly.

She looked up into his eyes as if to be surprised he had to ask.

"This was never going to be a fact finding mission, Lieutenant."

"But you know how hard we have worked for hundreds of years to circumvent major conflict? Could we not have at least tried to avoid it?"

"I can't see how. All I see right now is a small potential threat a long way from the Allied races' worlds. But if it is allowed to continue, it could become a big problem much closer to home. I will not allow that to happen."

"So we're here on a search and destroy mission?"

She didn't answer, but it was clear from the expression on her face that it was true.

"Now, those ships, do you believe them to be of the same origin as the one which attacked the Bulwark?"

"I...think so, but..."

"Speak plainly, Lieutenant."

"Same origin? I believe so, but they were...well. Small, a pushover compared to what we saw."

"You didn't have the power of a fleet at your side."

"And you weren't there," replied Santos.

"Commander, I don't mean to be rude. But if the thing that attacked us shows up again, you don't want to be here to see it."

"Lieutenant, if that thing turns up, then it will be

subjected to the same treatment it visited upon the Bulwark."

"I think you are underestimating the strength of what we are facing, Sir."

"Thank you, Lieutenant. Have your Company prepared for ground deployment."

"Yes, Sir," he replied, groaning as Santos followed him back across the bridge and out of earshot of the Commander.

"Do you think she wants war?"

"I don't think the Commander believes that is a possibility. She thinks this is just an isolated incident of some lost civilisation."

"And you know otherwise?"

Jones' eyes went wide as he stared at the Captain, but he would not give an answer.

"What are you not telling us?"

Jones shrugged. "I don't know anything for certain. All I know is you don't go meddling with something this powerful. Ever heard the meme 'don't poke the bear?'"

"No."

"It's an old saying, pretty self explanatory."

"Yeah, I got it. What are we really doing here?"

Jones was surprised to hear the Captain ask him, but he also knew a lot more than he was letting on.

"We've come to destroy the threat completely."

"And you think that can be achieved with this fleet?"

"No," he replied bluntly.

"So those ships that attacked us, what do you think they were?"

"The welcome party," he replied.

The view before them suddenly flickered and distorted

until the vast enemy vessel that had assaulted them before revealed itself. It blocked the path to the planet and filled the screen. Cohen's head snapped around and glared at Jones.

"Is that it?" she yelled.

"Yes," he replied, and he looked terrified.

He didn't know what he was expecting, but he prayed they wouldn't have to see it again. They could already see the charge building at the base of the mandibles protruding from the immense hull.

"We're getting hailed."

"Put them through," snapped Cohen.

The screen went black as it did before, and once again Jones could see what appeared as two eyes glowing in the darkness. It felt as though they were looking at him and growing wider with recognition. It was a sickening feeling to think he might be singled out, but there was no way he could tell for sure.

"I am Commander Cohen of the United Earth Navy and representative of the League of Four races. We do not come here with any hostile intentions, but we will defend ourselves when fired upon."

No response came.

"Resend that transmission in every language we have on record," she said to Nichols.

"Already done."

"What do you want from us?" Cohen asked.

They still weren't sure if they were even speaking to a sentient being or some kind of computer. But the motion of the lights appeared as eyes moving slightly before them, and it gave a sense of a living creature.

"What do you want from us?" she asked again.

Once again the transmission ended without a word, and they were left with the foreboding sight of the titanic vessel.

"What now?" Santos asked.

"Fire," replied Jones, "Don't wait, fire now while you still can."

Cohen hesitated, and just a few seconds later the energy reached the end of the maniples of the vast super weapon and joined. Cohen was speechless as she watched the beam of light burst out from the vessel and strike one of the destroyers off their port bow. The ship was blown apart into three pieces and smaller debris.

"All vessels engage target!" Cohen shouted, and her orders were quickly relayed.

The weapon systems once again opened fire, and they watched the screens as the fleet poured fire into the massive ship. They had no idea where or how to best target it, so they simply held position and opened up with everything they had. Bursts of energy from hidden weapon platforms aboard the enemy vessel opened fire on them, and for a moment it seemed the lone vessel was putting out as much fire as their entire fleet.

"Get us out of here...leave now while we still can!" Jones shouted at the Commander.

But she ignored him and turned back to the operations display.

"Have the Cholan vessels move to the stern of this thing and target its engines!"

Fire continued to pour into the ship, and they could feel the impacts at their feet as the whole ship was rocked by salvos from the mysterious craft. A light flashed before them, and Jones looked just in time to see the main gun blast another of the Human destroyers and destroy it in a single shot.

"We can't stay here. We can't beat this thing, Commander!"

"We must. Those are our orders," she snapped.

Jones looked past the Commander and could see a number of shadowy outlines growing nearer.

"What the hell is that?"

Nichols brought up a display to show it was a wing of small vessels. They looked too large to be fighters and nothing like the object that boarded them before. These were craft with stubby wings and possibly a cockpit. The nose was more like a mining drill than the front of an aircraft. Jones didn't know what was on board, but he knew just where they were heading.

"Do not let them reach us. Last time one of theirs got aboard, it nearly cost us all our lives."

"Direct forward batteries now," ordered Cohen.

The rain of fire obliterated two of the enemy craft, but another two passed within their firing solution and smashed into the hull of the Guam. Just as before, they felt no explosion, but warning lights and sirens flashed up on the hull breaches. Nichols was quick to direct the appropriate measures.

"Have we just been boarded?" Cohen asked.

Nichols was busy sealing off areas to patch up their hull.

"Have we been boarded?" she repeated in a stronger tone.

"I don't know."

Nichols was flicking through internal security monitors now. Several were not working, but they reached one that showed a ruined interior wall and part of the alien ship they had seen protruding through the breach. There was no movement for a second, but then what seemed like a double door slid inside the hull. Everyone watched out of mostly morbid curiosity and terror. They saw something move out into the light for just a moment. Nobody could tell what it was in the brief second they saw it, as the camera feed cut off.

"What the hell just happened?"

"Camera has been destroyed or deactivated," replied Nichols.

"Find another."

"They've been knocked out throughout most of the deck and elements above and below that position, Sir."

"Deploy drones, contain them!"

Nichols sent command orders on his screen to deploy the initial units.

"Let me go in," said Jones.

Cohen looked at him in surprise.

"You need eyes down there and someone to command the defence in person. You still have Captain Santos to hold and protect this position."

She quickly agreed and turned back to the battle before them. Jones rushed off the bridge and was glad to be able to do something rather than stand and watch helplessly as the fleet was torn apart. He raised his left arm and brought up the control orders for the Company he had been given. He sent the command for 1st Platoon to escort him and the others to his flanks.

Jones rushed into an elevator and hit the command for level five where he knew the enemy had breached. He was still alone when the doors closed, and he couldn't help but feel scared.

"Keep it together, keep it together," he whispered to himself.

He dropped the magazine from his rifle and pulled out another from his armour. He took one quick look to see it was filled with red tip armour piercing rounds, and then slammed it into the rifle. He knew they were not permitted for use about a ship, but he also knew they needed to survive.

He looked down at his compact and contour fit body armour. He'd always felt like a million credits in it, as he knew how much protection it provided against conventional weapons, but now knew how little it meant. About the only thing he could say for his equipment was that it was light and gave him great mobility.

The door to the elevator opened, and he found 1st Platoon waiting for him. Though they didn't make him feel any more comfortable or safe in the scenario. Having other Humans around gave a sense of safety, but the drones didn't provide the same factor. He knew it was purely psychological, but it still bothered him. The corridor ahead was broad and with only a few paths and doors off it. It reminded him of the urban combat training that he had practiced so many times, but he knew this was far worse. The ship was feeling like a dungeon now that he had to hunt some enemy far beyond their technology or understanding.

"1st Squad lead the way," he ordered, as he gave the command to the nearby platoons to close in on his console.

He had almost two hundred of the UEA's finest drones at his command, more than he'd ever had in his career. He clung to that fact now, in the hope that it would mask his fear and see some hope of victory.

Gunfire rang out to his right flank, and he looked down at his console. The lights flashed where one of his platoons had made contact. He clicked to get a video feed from one of the drones, but it was being jammed.

"Damn it," he said to himself and carried on with one of the squads in front. He used the drones to screen and protect himself, just as he had been trained. With all of the soldiers before him, he could not see ahead. Instead, he watched the feed from the drone on point from the console on his arm. It was like watching a video game, and yet the risk to his life made him feel otherwise.

The ambient lighting suddenly cut out without warning.

"Halt," he ordered, and the platoon came to a standstill.

Red emergency lighting cut in, and for a moment Jones felt relieved, but that soon failed also, and they were left in complete darkness.

"NVGs on," he ordered.

He pressed a button on his console, and a visor slid down from his helmet that dropped down to nose height. Lights flickered, and suddenly everything was illuminated with a three-colour palette and almost perfect visibility.

I hate these things.

He remembered when his failed during a night training exercise the year before. Lights flashed in the corridor up ahead, and he looked back down at his console. The camera feed dropped to the ground as the drone was hit. Jones leapt to the side of the corridor and took shelter in one of the large support beams running along the corridor. White flashes of energy zipped down the corridor and struck several of the drones. Jones saw two of the impacts blow the drones apart, but he saw another drop motionless from a lesser impact to the shoulder, as if it had simply been switched off.

He hunkered down in the cover and controlled his unit from his console. From the foremost drone's camera he could just make out the enemy up ahead, but the flashes of their weapons made it hard to get a bearing on exactly what he was seeing. The drones were returning fire with controlled bursts, but they seemed to have little effect on their attackers. He looked at the GPS positioning of his drones and could see 1st Squad was almost gone, with just two still in action. He directed 2nd Squad to move forward, and for 2nd Platoon to move in on their left flank from a parallel corridor.

2nd Squad went forward without fear or hesitation. They were nothing more than machines, but Jones could not help feel the loss when several more were cut down, and he wondered if they could make any progress.

"Ah, hell," he said and decided to weigh into the fray. He got up and peered around the pillar enough to get a view of the enemy. They were just twenty metres ahead. He raised his rifle, flicked the selector onto flash, and pulled the trigger. He looked away for just a moment but knew he didn't have to notify the squad beside him. They were programmed to block visuals when any friendly flash device was fired.

The whole corridor lit up with a flash of white light. A second later, Jones had his rifle up beside the pillar and was taking aim at the nearest enemy. He was surprised to see there appeared to be just three of them. They walked on four mechanical crab-like legs, but with more of a humanoid-shaped upper body. They appeared to be entirely mechanical. Each of their forearms was one of their devastating ranged weapons, but looked like little more than steel tubes. They appeared stunned for a moment, and Jones took his chance.

He aimed at the centre mass of the middle soldier and fired a single shot, but he heard it ricochet off its torso armour.

"No way," he whispered and fired another two shots, achieving nothing more. The drones were firing volleys into the creatures now but achieving nothing of note. They returned fire and destroyed another five drones in their opening salvo. Jones once again took aim at the head this time and fired. The shot glanced off, and now he was more terrified than ever. It was then he noticed a small glowing green light in its lower torso. It was as good a target to try as any. He took aim and fired a shot. The first did nothing, so he fired two more, and watched with joy as the soldier went limp and collapsed to the deck.

"All units, aim for the light in the lower torso. It's the only place we can get through."

The drones redirected their fire, but they were still having trouble getting through with regular ammunition. Despite this, he watched with relief as the remaining two enemy soldiers retreated down a nearby corridor.

"We've got the first wave on the run. All units close in and bring them down!"

2nd Squad went ahead, and he finally got out from cover and followed them. He went forward with a new found confidence. He could hear gunfire from the platoon to their left flank beginning to engage the two enemy soldiers that were running from them. He took a bend and found they had been cornered in the corridor between the two units and were firing wildly into both sides. He joined in the fight and started firing bursts into one of the creatures, but he couldn't get an accurate shot on the weak point he needed. They were moving back and forth firing so wildly.

Jones stopped firing and took careful aim, slowly tracking his target and waiting for his opportunity. He thought he had found his shot and began squeezing the trigger when a red pulse flashed from one of the enemy's weapons. It was so bright it blinded him for a split second. As he recovered, he noticed the ball of red light stop and erupt. It hit like a shockwave and launched him and the drones with him into the air. He was thrown two metres back, slammed into the deck, and slid until his shoulder smashed into one of the pillars.

He was stunned by the impact, but looking over from where he lay, a few of the drones were already back on their feet. Suddenly, a drone head flew past his field of vision, and he saw the two enemy soldiers cutting their way through. Metre-long blades were now protruding from the guns that they carried in place of arms. They cut and blasted their way through six drones before he could get to his feet. He activated his combat shield in the nick of time. Two rods extended out above and below his left arm, and a light green energy shield ignited around them.

A blade from one of the enemy soldiers hacked down at his shield. The impact of the blow drove him down onto one knee. But from there he placed the barrel of his rifle on the glowing bulb on the robot's torso and squeezed the trigger. Five shots ripped through its body. The Mech-like creature went limp and collapsed over him with what felt like the weight of a car.

Jones tried to move the body off him, but it was too heavy. He looked up and watched the other alien soldier cut through a drone with one of its blades. It then rose up on its rear legs and drove one of its front blades through another drone like a spear, piercing it from front to back. It landed back on all feet, taking aim with one of its arm-mounted cannons at Jones' head. All he had free was his right arm with the rifle still in his hand. He lifted it up with one hand and fired a burst in the desperate hope of doing something.

The first round slipped straight into the broad barrel opening of one of the cannons aimed at him, causing the energy inside to ignite. The soldier's arm was blown off and was thrown against the bulkhead on the far side. Jones was powerless to act any further, but watched five of his drones close in, keeping up the fire until finally the alien soldier slumped back down and was finished. Jones gave out a sigh of relief. He knew how lucky he had been.

"Get this thing off me!" he yelled.

The drones gathered around and managed to haul the dead soldier off him and help him to his feet. He coughed and spluttered, trying to get air back into his lungs and activated his comms link.

"This is Jones. We have engaged and neutralised three of the enemy. What is our status?"

"Lieutenant, we're getting out of here now. Should be at the gateway in less than a minute!" Santos shouted.

Jones could hear a mixture of frantic yelling and groans of pain in the background from wounded crewmembers.

"How many ships do we have left?"

"Not many," replied Santos wearily, "Have you cleared the ship of all hostile entities?"

"I don't know."

"Have the drones keep sweeping the ship, and get back

up here!"

Jones ran back towards the elevator and tapped in his orders into his console as he did so. He rushed in and hit the button. As the doors shut, he could feel liquid dripping down his face that he thought was sweat. He wiped his brow with the back of his hand, only to find to his horror that it was blood. His head was still throbbing from where he had been thrown hard onto the deck, but he didn't have time to check. He released the magazine from his rifle and let it drop to the floor of the elevator, slammed in a fresh one as the doors opened, and rushed back onto the bridge.

It was a scene of mayhem. The blast doors were buckled slightly, and one of the consoles had smoke belching out from it. A fire extinguisher was leaning against a panel nearby. Two crewmembers were being patched up from minor injuries, but most of all, his attention was drawn to the display screen. It showed the enemy vessel, but they were putting some distance between it. He knew they were heading for the gateway, and they had left a dozen crippled or destroyed ships in their wake.

Even as he was watching the screen, the Aranui ship was cut in two by the immense power of the enemy vessel. They all knew it was the most powerful ship they had taken into the system. They were running for their lives now, and everyone knew it.

"Can't we get any more power?" Cohen bellowed.

"We're at full capacity," replied Nichols.

The Commander turned back to watch the onslaught with Jones, knowing neither of them could do anything now. The last of the fighters were making rushed landings, and two blew up as they were hit from the smaller weapon systems of the enemy vessel.

"Did you use an EMP?"

"We used everything we had," replied Cohen solemnly.

Another Human ship between them and the enemy was blown apart just as they passed through into the gateway. They finally left the horrific sight of the enemy vessel behind. Cohen slumped into her chair without a word. Jones knew just how they felt, but he'd been through it the first time. More than anything, he was glad to be alive, and that was the overwhelming feeling in his head. He looked to Santos and could see he felt just the same way.

"We've got big trouble coming our way," said the Captain.

Jones could do nothing but nod in agreement.

CHAPTER FOUR

"We cannot risk more ships in a futile mission of aggression. The danger is in Kepler, almost five hundred light years away! I say we shut down the gateway and never return to that damned place again!"

Jones couldn't even be bothered to look up at who had made such a claim, as other civilian and military representatives waded into the argument. He was slumped in his seat, having not said a word for two hours. Once again he found himself amongst a heated debate, when he had signed up for adventure and the intrigue of exploration and maybe even combat. Now he asked himself why he bothered pursuing either. Gone were the illusions he had of what his career could be. He just wanted to go home and forget it all. Then he heard Jafar's voice silence the room, and so he looked up and paid attention.

"If a threat exists, then it will not remain contained within one system. We will have to deal with this danger, whether it is today, next month, or next year," he stated.

"And how do you know that?" asked one of the

Human representatives, "We have already heard from those who were there, and that all this started when our forces trespassed on alien ground. Maybe they just want to be left alone?"

The man appeared to be in his mid-forties and spoke with a Scandinavian accent. He was completely bald and looked flustered from the whole debate. The display in front of him read 'MUEN Bylund', a minister of the United Earth Nations.

Jafar shook his head.

"Whatever you believe, you should prepare for war, because it is coming whether you will it or not."

The room fell silent until President Isaacs broke the silence. He was here in person this time, and everyone knew how severe the situation must be for so many key officials to be physically in one room together.

"Governor Irala, what do you think?"

Everyone turned to the alien, but no response came.

"You lost people out there, too. Numbers you cannot afford to lose with such a small population. You must have some feelings towards this?"

"We did not send any Aranui on your operation to Kepler," he replied sternly.

"How do you mean?"

"My people cannot afford to risk our lives. We sent a ship to escort your mission only."

"So you let our people take the hit? You let thousands of Humans, Krys, and Cholans die?" Byland asked.

"When you have a population so small it could fit on a single capitol ship, you would be cautious, too."

It was hard to disagree.

"Did you believe the alien presence on Kepler could be

a threat?" Isaacs asked.

"Yes," he replied.

"And did you know this threat existed before we first made contact?"

"That they were inhabiting Kepler-186f, no. That they existed? Yes."

Many in the room gasped at the response. The room then erupted into a multitude of frenzied arguments. Jones rubbed his sore head as he felt it continue to throb, though he wondered how much the current meeting was to blame for that. He could see he was no longer needed. He got up and tried to make his way out quietly while the argument ensued, but as he got a few paces from his chair, he heard the President bellow.

"Lieutenant Jones!"

He stopped dead, and the room fell silent again. Now he felt like a fool, so he simply stood where he had stopped and turned to face the President.

"Lieutenant. We can argue this position for many more hours, but let's hear it from you. A man who was on the ground and with firsthand experience during both engagements. What would you do in our position? Given the combined power of the League of Races, how would you tackle this problem?"

"Problem, Sir?"

"What would you call it?"

"Pandora's Box, Sir. A powder keg...a disaster."

The President grimaced at every one of his words. It was the sort of plain speaking language that simply didn't get used in his world of politics.

"Okay, where would you go from here?"

"Sir. I would look to our history. We cannot leave such

a dire threat to continue to exist. If a threat exists, it must be dealt with. We need more ships, better weapons, and the soldiers to wield them. We must gear up for war, and ensure we hit this with everything we can before our chance is gone."

"War? Is that your only answer to a problem?" Bylund asked. He turned to the President, "Mr President, you cannot ask a fighting man to make a choice between peace and war, for he is only invested in one of those options."

Isaacs ignored the Minister and turned to Irala who still seemed to have more to offer.

"Governor, do you support the Lieutenant's appraisal of the situation?"

Irala nodded. "If our records are correct, it is the Morohta who you have encountered; an ancient race that scoured the universe and destroyed all who they met. They will come for us, and they will mercilessly destroy everything in their path."

Everyone in the room was trying to take in what Irala had just said, and Isaacs opened his mouth to speak when two Cholan advisors rushed into the room and to the side of their representative, Ambassador Ucan. Jones almost laughed at the sight of the Cholans darting across the room. They looked like children that were simply out of proportion and then dressed up to be adults. They all knew it must be important for them to barge in, and waited on Ucan to share whatever vital information was with them.

Finally, the Cholan Ambassador stood up. He was as short as the rest of them and wore a dark red suit that was more of Earth fashion than his own people. He looked distraught and unable to frame his words.

"What is it, Ambassador?" Isaacs asked.

"I...I have just received confirmed reports that our frontier colony of Coba has come under attack, and we have lost contact."

"Attacked? By who?"

"One of our ships managed to transmit this signal before it was destroyed."

Ucan held out a small remote control and pressed a key that projected a screen. They were looking at a vividly coloured nebula, and lights flashed within it like a storm. The lights grew brighter, and the view began to clear. They could just make out the outline of a ship, one that Jones was now all too familiar with.

"No," he whispered to himself, feeling his whole body go rigid with fear.

The weapon system of the alien ship fired a burst of light towards the video source, and the signal was lost.

"It's begun," said Jafar.

Isaacs turned to Irala for answers.

"You seem to know a whole lot more about this new race, so tell us, what should we do?"

"Not a new race, but a very old one. There is not a place in the universe you can go that they will not find you. Fight or die."

"Fight?" Isaacs asked in amazement, "We haven't had to fight a real war in generations. We don't have that capacity."

"But you did," replied Jafar.

"Yes, a long time ago, but those days are gone, and so are the Humans who lived and survived it."

"They're not all gone," he replied casually.

"What do you mean?"

"When humanity once stood on the brink of

destruction, a worse time than you have ever known in your history, one man stood above all else and saw you to victory. He is not dead. He is just forgotten."

"No, no, no," Jones joined in, "You can't be serious. He's talking about Mitch Taylor."

"The marine?" Isaacs asked, "My history is a little rusty, but wasn't he a total head case?"

"He was my friend," Jafar said firmly.

"And mine, I am proud to say," added Irala.

Jafar went on, "Mitch Taylor is still alive in suspended animation back on Earth. With the technology you have today, the willpower and effort, you could bring him back to us."

"And what would that achieve? We just lost thousands of personnel in Kepler. Wars aren't won by one man, what difference can this one Human make?"

"I must protest," stated Jones, "Taylor is of a bygone era. We have moved past those horrific times of war."

"I thought so," said Isaacs.

Jafar continued. "What difference can one man make to such a massive threat? I have often wondered the same. I never could say what made Mitch Taylor so incredibly special. I believe he was, as you say, more than the sum of his parts. Taylor achieved greatness. He wrestled victory from an enemy when there seemed no hope. He made all the difference. We need men like him in a time like this."

Everyone waited for some further thought or comment from the President. Bylund could no longer hold himself back and broke the silence.

"We've got real problems to deal with here, and you are giving serious consideration to expending substantial money and resources to bring back a man who should have died in his own time hundreds of years ago. Let's focus on the task at hand."

Isaacs raised his hand for silence.

"We must indeed deal with the threats before us, but Lord Jafar raises a worthy point. Humanity has been at peace for so long that we have forgotten how to wage war."

"And that is a good thing," snapped Bylund.

The President glared at him before going on.

"We do need to move on to other matters. But I trust in Lord Jafar's advice on this matter, and we need all the help we can get."

"But Mr President…" pleaded Bylund.

"No!" boomed Isaacs, "I will not waste time arguing on this matter. I was elected into this position, and I will damn well act on my responsibility while I still hold this office. However, I will spend no more time on this. Lieutenant Jones?"

"Yes, Sir?"

"As President of the League, I am personally ordering you to manage the Taylor situation. I know your ancestors have history with him, and that may work in your favour."

"Mr President, I am not remotely qualified for this."

"None of us are. Lieutenant, we have a lot of work to do, work that you cannot do. I am asking you to manage this. Will you do this for me?"

"Yes, yes, of course, Sir."

"Thank you, Lieutenant. My assistants will ensure you have everything you need. Now, if you will excuse us, we have a lot more to discuss."

Jones was glad to be given his leave of absence, but he wished it had been under other circumstances. He stepped out of the room and passed several ranks of security officials from all four races. He found Cynara sitting there, waiting for him.

"You're still here?"

She laughed. "Nice to see you, too."

She stood up to walk with him as he continued past.

"So really, how are you still here?"

"I've been given leave. Your husband almost dying twice ensured that for me."

"I almost die, and it's you who gets time out?"

"Guess so. And I've got a shuttle at my disposal. I'm all yours. Where are we heading?"

"Earth," he replied quickly.

"Great, be nice to take some vacation time there."

"We're not going there to rest. We have work to do."

She looked puzzled. "So where are we heading?"

"Paris."

* * *

"Beautiful isn't it?" Cyn asked.

Jones was looking down from the co-pilots seat of their shuttle as they made their final descent. There was woodland and gardens for kilometres in every direction. They could see the city far into the distance, but where they were about to land was serene. Not a single other aircraft was in sight, for only those with clearance were allowed to take to the skies there.

"You know the city used to stand right here?"

"Yes, but you still haven't told me what we're doing here?"

"Following orders," he replied bluntly.

She shook her head and turned back to the controls to make a landing in the nearest small opening to the coordinates Will had given her. They put down smoothly, and he was quickly out the door. They both stepped a few paces onto the grass, stopping to take it all in.

This was not the artificial garden he had seen on the Ares station. Everything was natural here. Trees reached high into the sky; the grass cut short, and everything in sight was so well cared for it almost appeared artificial. He'd never appreciated the smell of nature as much as this day. He thought back to the confines of the Guam when he thought he would be trapped and killed in any second.

But then Jones looked down at his console and quickly took to a stride towards the coordinates he had been given.

"I don't understand this, Will. Are we working or not?"

"We're working all right, just on the last thing I could ever have expected to do."

They passed through several hedgerows and came to an opening inside a circle of dense and tall trees. As they went inside, they could see an old stone structure and stepped closer. It had the statue of a man on top of it.

"What? What is this?" Cyn asked.

"Resting place of Mitch Taylor."

"The Mitch Taylor?"

"Yep."

"I don't understand; what are we doing here?"

"Bringing him back from the dead."

She was speechless, as he led her around the structure where they found several soldiers with drones and medical personal waiting at the sealed doorway to the structure.

"Lieutenant Jones?" one of them asked.

"Yes," he replied.

"We are about to begin. Do we have your permission?"

"Proceed."

Cyn looked at everything around her and couldn't understand what was going on, but before she could say a word, the doorway released and slid open. They walked into the chamber to find a frozen incubation chamber. She could see equipment all around him that seemed to be working. She had expected to find nothing but a coffin.

"He's alive?"

"Only barely."

"What are you doing with him?"

"My orders. Bring him back, and prepare him to fight."

"What? That's crazy."

"Yes, it sounds that way to me. No, it is crazy. But it's just the kind of crazy that you might expect with Taylor."

She reached down to his hand and held it tight.

"Will. I know you feel attached to the whole history of your family and those wars, but why are you doing this?"

"This isn't me. I never wanted this. These are my orders."

He looked over to the medical staff.

"How long until he is ready for departure?"

"We can have the chamber loaded aboard your shuttle within the hour."

* * *

Seven days later.

Taylor awoke and took in a deep breath of air as if he had just awoken from a nightmare. He sat up quickly but felt pain from the sudden movement, and then tightness in his chest. He was almost blinded from the bright light overhead and reached down to feel scar tissue on his chest. He looked down to see precise incision marks running almost the length and width of his torso, and other scars that appeared less uniform and more injury related. As he touched the wounds, his memory flashed back to his final fight with Erdogan, and his pulse began to race as he remembered the enemy's blade piercing his chest.

His vision was adapting to the light now, and he looked around to see he was in a medical facility and sitting on a bed in a small room. He didn't recognise much of the equipment around him, but he never had paid that much attention to hospitals.

"Anyone around?" he asked, his voice croaky, "Anybody? Where's my uniform?"

The door opened, and an officer approached with two medical staff. The officer wore a bizarre-looking uniform that appeared comical and corny to Taylor.

"Where the fuck are you from? Some shit hole to make you dress like that."

The medical staff were astonished by how he spoke, but that was no surprise to him. The officer only smiled; he was the only other person in the room who understood the language of the twenty-second century man.

"You'll forgive these doctors. They are not accustomed to such vulgar dialogue. My name is Lieutenant Jones."

"Vulgar, what the fuck?"

Jones only smiled once again.

"Jones? I knew a Jones once, not so long back," he said, thinking back to his best friend.

"Yes you did, but further back than you realise, Colonel."

Taylor didn't know what he meant and looked confused.

"I am Lieutenant Jones of the 2nd Airborne Regiment,

previously known to you as the Parachute Regiment of the United Kingdom. Captain Charlie Jones, your friend, is my ancestor."

Taylor began to see some resemblance in the man now, although he looked a less sturdy and strong man than his friend.

"What? Ancestor?"

"Colonel, do you remember your last engagement?"

"Against that bastard…Erdogan? Fucking right I do. We nailed him good and proper."

"And do you remember how severe your injuries were from that battle?"

Taylor's right hand instinctively reached down to the wounds on his chest, and he remembered it perfectly.

"Like it was yesterday."

"For you, it was. But you were mortally wounded in that battle, Colonel. You should not have survived it, but the decision was made to put you into suspended animation to save your life, and perhaps one day bring you back."

"One day? How long has it been?"

Jones took in a deep breath and tried to understand for himself how the news would feel. He could hold back the truth no longer and simply came out with it.

"Almost four hundred years."

Taylor didn't know what to say. He tried to think what that would mean for him, but it was beyond comprehension.

The doors opened once again, and a US Marine General strode in. The uniform had changed, but the insignia had not. He was a short and thin man in his early sixties, well tanned, and with a receding hairline.

"Colonel Taylor, I am General Fin. I am here to oversee your recovery and reinstatement."

"Sir, can I have a word with you?" Jones asked.

"Yes, certainly."

They moved to step outside, but Taylor soon piped up.

"Hey, assholes, anything you have to say about this happens right here where I can see and hear it. You tell me four hundred years have passed, and expect me to just jump when you say jump?"

Jones shrugged and the General continued.

"Taylor. What you achieved in your time was quite simply amazing, but those days have gone. You're a dinosaur, a relic of a bygone era that we are all glad to have seen gone. I never agreed to this operation, and I have voiced my concerns. Nonetheless, here we are. When we need young and fit fighting men, we get an ancient wreck that knows nothing about civilised society. I know all about you, Taylor. You jumped ships more times than I care to count, and you lived only to fight. There's no place for men like you in this world, Taylor. But that doesn't matter, you'll screw this up all on your own, and I'll be there ready for when they want to put you back on ice."

He turned and strode out of the room just as quickly as he had come in.

"He speaks like I'm some kind of criminal. Has the whole world gone to shit while I've been away?"

"Far from it. We've just evolved a little."

"Yeah, evolved into a new kind of asshole."

"I'm sorry, Colonel. I can see this is a lot to take in. I am going to give you a few hours. You have access to any news or history you want. You can reach me directly on your console," he said, pointing to the large watch-like object wrapped around Taylor's arm.

He turned to leave, but Taylor stopped him.

"So this is it? I'm on ice, and you bring me back now? Why now? Everyone I ever knew is gone. Why did you even bother?"

"Honestly, I don't know why, but somebody you used to know fought to get you out."

"Who?"

"Lord Jafar."

Taylor was speechless.

"You've got twelve hours. Then I'll be back."

* * *

Taylor pulled on the uniform that had been laid out for him. It was the same awful design he had seen Jones wearing, but it was all he had. Exactly to the minute, Jones arrived.

"Good," said Jones, "Follow me."

Taylor did so, but there was no enthusiasm in his stride. He wondered why he was even alive. He grabbed hold of Jones' arm and pulled him around firmly, so he could look into his eyes.

"Lieutenant, don't bullshit me now. You know this whole situation is a load of crap. Why did you wake me, and what do you want from me?"

"Okay…we're in big trouble. Kind of trouble when you do anything to try and dig your way out… that's you."

"Trouble? Krys invaded again?"

"No. Most of the Krys live under local rule in their own sector, with a fair share on Earth. This is a new threat, something none of us have seen before. Not even Councillor Irala has seen these in his lifetime."

"Irala is still alive, too?"

"You see, two people you know. This threat, it's bigger and nastier than anything you can ever have imagined."

"I can imagine quite a bit, seen even more than I can imagine."

"This isn't about Earth, anymore, Taylor. This is bigger than one world. It's about the survival of four races and countless colonies across multiple star systems. I will give it to you straight, Colonel. I don't think waking you up was a good idea, and I don't think you have anything to add to our cause. I can provide valuable resources at the frontline; instead, I am stuck here babysitting a relic. I have a great admiration for what you achieved, but that's history."

"All right, I get it, you don't like me. Join the list, but stop bullshitting me, and tell me what you really want from me."

Jones grimaced as if not wanting to say but finally came out with it.

"The President of the colonies is quite taken with the idea of you making a comeback, and with Jafar and Irala in your corner, he has made that happen. They think you can make a difference. In honour of your past achievements, you are being given command of twenty of the finest men and women of the US Marine Corps and the 2nd Airborne Regiment."

"An Inter-Allied unit?"

"Yes, I knew you'd like that; nostalgia and all that. This may be a great trip down memory lane for you, but lives are at stake. I say you are a waste of time, but I'd be happy to be proven wrong."

"Would you?" Taylor asked sarcastically.

"Yes," he snapped.

"Twenty men? What on Earth am I supposed to do

with twenty men?"

Jones continued to lead the way and stepped through an exterior door that eventually led them out into the open air. Hover vehicles soared past them and others far above.

"Welcome to New York, Colonel, the largest Marine and Naval base in the United States."

They kept on walking until they came to a drill square where hundreds of soldiers stood in line awaiting them. One of the nearby marines called them to attention, but Taylor did not even stop. He strolled right up and continued on down the line. The front rank was made up of an even mix of marines and paras as Jones had said, but he stopped in his tracks on realising everything behind them was robotic. Humanoid robots.

"What the fuck are those?" he asked.

One of the marines in front of him laughed. Taylor looked at the rank on his shoulder. He was a Lieutenant, and his nametag read 'Watkins.'

"Something funny?"

The officer couldn't seem to wipe the grin off his face. Without any warning at all, Taylor's fist punched into the man's stomach, causing him to keel over.

"Colonel Taylor!" Jones shouted.

Taylor looked up with scorn at Jones; giving him such a glare he did not dare go any further.

"Get back up!" he yelled at Watkins.

He turned his attention back to Jones.

"What the hell is this? Twenty men and a bunch of what, robots?"

"Combat drones, the latest and most advanced currently in service."

"Drones? To replace men?"

"To save the lives of men," said Jones.

Taylor looked back to see every one of the Humans before him held the rank of Lieutenant.

'Where are the ORs?"

"Handling other duties. ORs do not fulfil combat roles. Drone squads are led by officers, same in every army on Earth."

"Not anymore, they're not."

"Colonel, these are advanced combat drones that are tried and tested."

"This war has only just begun, and you're already losing, right?"

Jones couldn't bear to agree, but he knew it was true.

"You brought me back because the new ain't working. Time for a little of the old."

He strode up to him so that he could whisper in his ear.

"You listen to me, Lieutenant. You might think you're here to babysit me, but you would be wrong. Give me command and a group of troops, and those troops are mine, and that goes for you, too. You better get used to that."

He turned back to the unit.

"Have those…things leave us. Dismiss them, now!" he shouted.

He watched as they all hurriedly tried to punch in controls, and the drones marched away into a nearby warehouse. Taylor stepped right up in front of Watkins who winced as he did so. Taylor reached up for the chrome Lieutenant bar on the man's right shoulder and ripped it off of his uniform and tossed it aside.

"Someday a few of you might achieve the rank of officer, if you live that long, but from now on you are all busted to Private."

Jones gasped, but Taylor glared at him once more.

"Except you, Lieutenant, you're my number two. The rest of you, get those ranks off your uniforms, right now!"

Not one of them hesitated to do so after seeing the brutal treatment of Watkins. Taylor wasn't sure whether to be glad of their acceptance of his command, or angry for how easily they folded.

"Right now you probably hate me? Good. I don't know what you think you know about my history, and I don't much care. I have only two things to achieve here. I have to make you into the best goddamn fighters there are, and then I have to keep you alive to keep on fighting. Everything we do from now on will be to that end. I am not cruel. I will not make you do anything that I do not consider absolutely vital. I once commanded the most elite infantry Regiment on Earth. To me that was yesterday, to you, it's history you probably never even learned. I expect you to meet that standard. Gear up, full combat load out. You have thirty minutes. Fall out!"

They did so without hesitation, but Jones was still shaking his head.

"You're awake a day, and you're causing this much trouble. You know Watkins has never taken a punch in his life?"

"Yeah? Well, now he has. You learn through experience. Next time he'll take it better."

"Next time?"

"You get hit in combat and you aren't conditioned for it, aren't ready for it, you'll go down like a cheap hooker. Train, fight, harden the fuck up, and you stay on your feet and keep going."

Jones shook his head.

"You expect to pick up right where you were, but we aren't that kind of people anymore, Taylor."

"Bullshit. So you became pussies for a little while. You had no reason to be otherwise. My generation fought so that you didn't have to, and you've slacked ever since. You think I don't understand this, but I went through the same. You seem to know some of my history, but you don't know what it was like to see an alien for the first time and realise you can barely hurt it. Line up a squad of marines with the finest hardware on offer and just bounce right off. I was scared shitless, and I won't deny it, but do you know how that feels?"

Jones went silent for a moment, and Taylor could see the fear in his eyes as he flashed back to recent events. His expression seemed to change entirely.

"You do, don't you?"

"First contact, I was there. Barely survived the experience."

"Well, I'll be damned, there is a fighter amongst you," Taylor replied, smiling, "You kill one of them?"

Jones nodded, but there was still fear in his eyes.

"How'd you do it?"

"I...I drew it into an escape pod...and I...I jettisoned the pod with two grenades inside."

"Woohoo! You might just be a real Jones yet!" Taylor hollered.

Jones couldn't understand where his enthusiasm was coming from, and yet he was drawn to Taylor's electrifying personality, nonetheless.

The twenty men and women formed up soon after. Taylor paced up and down looking at their equipment.

They wore full body compression suits with slimline form fitting body armour plates over most key parts of the body.

"This armour, it any good?"

"It will withstand a Reitech 8.1mm round at ten metres. Shrapnel, blunt trauma, and abrasion," replied Jones.

Taylor smiled; realising Reitech was still around as an entity.

"But will it stop whatever the enemy is firing at you?"

"Our shields can withstand a couple of shots at best, but our armour has done little to protect us."

"These suits of yours, do they provide any boost in power or strength, speed?"

Jones shook his head.

"Close quarter weaponry?"

"We do not carry any. It serves no purpose today."

"No purpose when you have nobody to fight!"

He paced up and down the line.

"I guess most of you would laugh to hear that in my day when the rifles failed, or we were in too close, we used small sword or spear-like weapons, and full shields, not retractable. And we fought in exoskeleton suits to boost the abilities of our bodies. What have you got? Minimal ballistic protection and a fancy folding shield?"

He stopped before the largest man in the unit. He stood ten centimetres taller than Taylor but was of similar build. His nametag read 'Antos.'

"Give me your rifle," he ordered.

The man quickly complied, and Taylor took ten paces back before throwing the rifle behind him.

"Private Antos. I am the enemy. Your rifle has just been dropped. There is nowhere to run except through me. Are you up to the task?"

Antos looked to his comrades in shock.

"Private, you are a British Para. To me that means something; it means you are one of the toughest sons of bitches in the galaxy. Prove it. Get to that rifle."

Taylor stood squarely in front of the weapon as the man approached. He looked cautious and as if he had never fought with his own hands before. Taylor shook his head in disbelief at the sight. Antos seemed wary of attacking, or scared to.

"Come on! Hit me!" Taylor ordered.

The man lunged forward with a quick but clumsy strike. Taylor parried the strike off to one side and drove his knee up into the man's abdomen. The armour took much of the impact, but it still shocked him. Taylor then grabbed Antos' lead arm and pulled him off balance, driving his elbow into the man's shoulder blade as he was thrown face first onto the hard parade ground floor and pinned in position. Taylor pulled his arm back against the leverage of his elbow, just enough that he was wincing in pain, but not enough to dislocate it.

He let go, helped Antos up, and handed him his rifle.

"This won't do at all. Not at all!" Taylor shouted, "I am going to make fighters out of all of you, and you are going to earn that uniform you wear!"

He looked back to Jones.

"Lieutenant, you have them. I want a ten klick run. Take a time."

"In full combat equipment?"

"This is what you go to war in, is it not?" he yelled back.

The Lieutenant agreed.

"Right face! By the left, quick march!"

Taylor watched them trudge off into the distance and

shook his head.

"This is gonna be a lot of work."

CHAPTER FIVE

Taylor rode along through the base aboard one of the hover vehicles he had seen earlier. It was large enough for six personnel and their gear, and yet the compact engines and whatever provided the lift were concealed well beneath the framework. It resembled a flying sand rail buggy to him. His driver was a young Hispanic woman. She looked like she was barely out of school and yet held the rank of Lieutenant. She had told him her name, but he hadn't been paying attention.

They were passing along lines of houses now. Each one of them was cube shaped and appeared as though made from smoked glass. The buildings looked lavish in size and even had gardens.

"What rank do you have to be to get this life of luxury?" Taylor asked his driver.

"Each one of these properties is provided to all recruits who gain a commission, Sir," she said in surprise.

"All combat personnel are officers, and all officers live like this? Must be a pretty small Corps these days."

"Yes, Sir. We have been streamlined and rely heavily on automated and autonomous machines. It must be a far cry from the Marine Corps you once knew. We have a wealth of equipment to make our work easier today that I bet you could only dream of having access to, back when you could have done with it."

Taylor laughed.

"What is it, Colonel?"

"I could have done with all this junk? Coming from a society that has dug me out from storage and dusted me off because it can't cope when the shit hits the fan."

"I'm not sure what you mean, Colonel."

He wasn't sure if she was being politely oblivious or genuinely ignorant of their situation, but it brought a smile to his face anyway. They finally came to a standstill at house number 452.

"This is it," she stated.

Taylor got out and approached the front door. The structure was spartan and uninspiring to look at, though highly functional. As he got a few metres away, the door slid open.

"Welcome home, Mitch," said a voice from a hidden speaker near the doorway.

"What the hell is that?"

"Sir, the entrance is programmed to recognise your body language, voice, and retina. It will lock and unlock as necessary."

"Great," he added sarcastically, "Another useless piece of tech."

"Is there anything more I can do for you, Colonel?"

He turned back and looked down at the name on her uniform. 'Rocha.'

"Ever seen any action, Rocha?"

"Over one hundred combat simulations. A dozen zero G exercises, another…"

She stopped as she saw Taylor shake his head.

"You can do all the training in the world, Lieutenant. In fact you should, but that isn't what I asked. You want to do what a marine was born to do, you show up tomorrow and sign up with me."

"I…I can't."

"Can't? You are a Marine Lieutenant. I don't want to hear you can't do anything. Be there tomorrow morning. Lose that bar. Come and join me, Rocha, and I'll make you a marine. Get you out from behind that wheel, ferrying around officers you don't care about."

"Sir, I like this job."

"Goddamn it. You know how long women fought to get frontline duties in the Corps? And now you're happy being a butler with a Corps uniform. Have a little pride, Rocha. Come with me. I can't promise you safety, career advancement, or a great retirement package. But I can offer you the chance to be a marine, a real marine."

"Sir, I can't be part of your operation, not without authorisation, and that will never happen…I just…"

"Just turn up tomorrow morning and be ready to get to work. I'll handle the rest."

He turned and strode into his new accommodation. It was a spacious open plan lower floor with a small elevator on one wall being the only means of going up to the higher floor. He shook his head at it all.

"Lazy," he said to himself.

The ground floor was laid out like a show house, but it was also stark. There was not a single item of his inside.

As the door to the house closed behind him, his situation truly dawned on him. He had leapt right back into his life as a marine, but now he was finally alone without something to occupy his mind, it began to wander to all that was now missing in his life. He thought of Eli, even though she had been lost a long time before the end of the war. He remembered losing so many friends, to the level he thought he had lost everything. But now, alone, and with not a single recognisable face, he was starting to appreciate how much he truly had left before the end.

The room was completely silent, and that did not help with the emptiness Taylor now felt. He staggered over to the sofa in the middle of the room and slumped down into it with a sigh. As he came to a rest, a screen appeared. It was two metres wide by a metre high and projected just off the wall in front of him. On the display was merely the picture of an envelope, but a voice soon joined it.

"Mitch Taylor, you have fifty-seven messages in archive."

Taylor looked scornfully at the screen. He expected they would be nothing more than advertising and other crap he wasn't interested in dealing with. He looked around for something, anything to spark his imagination or give him something to do, but there was nothing. So he got up and went to the kitchen. He looked in the cupboards and only found prepared meals that looked far from appetising. He then opened up the fridge to find flavoured water and energy drinks.

"Where the hell do you get a beer around here?"

To his amazement the voice that had greeted him at the door answered his question.

"Alcoholic beverages are not permitted within the

confines of the base."

"Fucking great," he muttered.

He grabbed a bottle of the flavoured water and scowled at it as he opened it and wandered back over to the sofa. To his surprise it actually tasted good, but he wasn't going to admit it. He was all too aware that he had no connection to this world. There was nobody he knew to talk to, and nothing for him to do until the next day of training commenced.

What the hell am I doing here?

He felt unsettled and a little sick. Last thing he remembered was dying and knowing everything that needed to be was resolved. He had defeated Erdogan, and he had nominated a successor that would see peace amongst the races. But that was all gone now. He felt completely lost in the world. He had nobody to turn to and nothing to occupy his mind. He was starting to wonder why he was even alive.

"Oh, what the hell, play the first message," he said.

The screen lit up, and he was amazed to see Coco standing in her full dress uniform. She was in front of some kind of monument, but he didn't recognise it, not until he noticed his name in the background. Tears rolled down her face, and she didn't speak for a moment. To Taylor it seemed like just a few days ago that he had seen the widow of his best friend. He remembered how she expressed her love for him after her husband, and his best friend, had died - Charlie Jones. She wept for a few more seconds, but it brought a smile to his face to see her.

"Here we are," she finally said, pointing to his tomb behind her. Her thick French accent was adorable as always, "Of all the people who died, I thought you would be one to make it through," she said as she wept once again. "You did it, Mitch. You saved us all," she said as she tried to wipe the tears from her face. "I know that one day you will return to us, but I fear it will not be in my lifetime. You were good to me, Mitch, and I just wanted to give something back. When you finally wake up, I want you to make the most of your life. You deserve it. You fought for it, and you gave everything so that we could live on. When you see this, know that it is your time. I cannot do anything more for you in life, but I will record a new message for you every year when I visit, I promise. Good luck, Mitch, and thank you."

The message ended and Taylor was frozen. He didn't know what to think or how to respond to that. His head was started to ache, trying to get his head around the time lapse between the video and where he was now. It was like a bad dream. Her words echoed in his mind until he was overwhelmed with a will to live. He could not bear to disappoint her even though she would never know.

"You thought we fought for this peace? Well it didn't last," he said quietly, "But that's why I'm here. I wasn't born to live in peace, no matter how much I want it. They locked me up for good. Might as well have put a sign on my tomb saying 'break and enter only in case of pending invasion.' Well they need me now, god help them, because they've got me for good now, and they're not gonna like it."

He smiled, knowing he had a purpose in life and a reason to go on living.

* * *

Taylor strode back to the drill square where he had left his new unit the day before, but this time he had one of the Krys at his side, who was also a member of the Marine Corps. They were formed up and waiting for him. He paced along the line, noting that every single one of them had removed their ranks except for Jones, as he had ordered. Many of them looked at the alien with suspicion, not because they were inherently suspicious of the Krys, but because of what Taylor might have them do. All were in full combat load out. He strode up to Jones who stood three metres in front of the troops.

"You're time?" Taylor asked.

"Sixty-seven minutes."

Taylor laughed.

"Over an hour for ten klicks? This isn't the Air Force, Lieutenant. I expect better."

"Sir, they are exhausted. We never run in full gear, and there is no need for it, anyway. We are a motorised force."

"Really? No need for it? You think I'm wasting your time here, don't you, Lieutenant?"

"I do, Sir. I respect what you did back in your day. But that was then, and this is now. I am needed up there for whatever we are about to face, and instead I'm stuck down here pandering to you, a relic of a bygone era."

Taylor smiled.

"Well at least you found the balls to speak plainly."

He turned around to address the rest of them when he saw a vehicle draw up nearby. Rocha leapt out and strode up towards him.

"Private Rocha reporting for duty, Sir."

"Your CO let you sign up with me just like that?"

"Sir, he said if I was foolish enough to go, and you were

stupid enough to take me, yes."

"Then you're in for one hell of a ride, Private. Fall in."

He turned back to the unit as she joined their ranks. Many were still looking suspiciously at the Krys marine beside Taylor.

"I bet you all think you are serious bad asses. You're from two of the best fighting units the world has to offer, or certainly used to be."

"Antos? You're a big bastard. What do you do when you meet an enemy who's bigger, stronger, and tougher than you are?"

Antos looked confused as Taylor looked over to the alien.

"This is Babacan," he said to introduce him, "As a training exercise, we are going to assume for a moment that Babacan here is an enemy combatant. Antos, step forward."

He did so without hesitation.

"An alien combatant stands before you. He wants to tear your head off, what do you do?"

"Shoot him, Sir."

A few of the others chuckled at the response, and even Taylor smiled. He stepped forward.

"Yes, and when you run out of ammunition. When your gun is lost or damaged in combat, what do you do then?"

Antos shrugged.

"Give me your rifle, Private," Taylor ordered.

The man begrudgingly obliged.

"In my day we learned two very important facts very quickly, one, the Human body is not strong enough when faced with such a powerful opponent, and two, only a fool goes into combat without a weapon he can depend on to save his life, when you're down in the dirt and having to fight with your own two hands. Antos, Babacan here is going to kill you unless you can stop him. Begin."

"But, Colonel, we don't fight the other races. We don't even compete with them in sport. It's not fair game."

"Fair? I haven't seen a fair fight in war, Private, and neither will you. Begin!"

Anton put his hands up into boxing stance. It was clear he had fighting knowledge, but he still looked terrified. Babacan rushed at him. The alien stood a head taller and substantially heavier in build. He swung a heavy hook for Antos' head, but he managed to just duck under and delivered an uppercut to the alien's stomach. The impact barely seemed to shake the creature, and he twisted back, smashing Antos' cheek with a backfist that sent him hurling several paces until gaining his balance.

Blood was dripping from the man's mouth, and yet the fear seemed to have gone, and he was now taking it seriously. He went forward and struck two quick jabs into Babacan's stomach before using a low kick to the alien's lead leg, but it did not strike with enough power to topple him. Babacan kicked hard into Antos' stomach, causing him to be launched off his feet and land hard on his back. Even as he was falling, the alien was leaping towards him with the intent to land a punch that would flatten his skull to the ground below.

"Halt!" Taylor yelled.

The alien landed over the top of Antos. Neither he nor Taylor was sure if Babacan would have gone all the way, and that was terrifying to the Private. But Babacan opened up his huge clenched fist, offered his hand to the man, and hauled him to his feet.

"The first time I ever fought a Krys warrior in close quarters it nearly ended me. The fact is they have an edge over us genetically. They are bigger, stronger, more resilient to pain, and tougher. Now I can't tell you what it is we might have to face, but if Lieutenant Jones' reports are anything to go by, you can be sure it won't be easy."

"Antos is the strongest one here. If he can't win, what are we supposed to do?" asked one of the female troopers.

Taylor strolled over to the woman. She stood as tall as him and looked quite masculine, especially compared to Rocha who had just joined them.

"And you are?"

"Bailey, Sir."

"Well, Bailey. We have to make up for our deficiencies. Some of that can be achieved in superior training, but the reality is, we need to be physically stronger than our bodies were intended to be, and we must be armed with weapons that allow us to fight in close quarters."

"You're talking about hand-to-hand combat?" she asked, almost speechless, "You want us to fight like Vikings, hacking and slashing our way through our enemies, when we have access to the best ballistic weaponry ever made?"

"And when those wonders of ballistic technology fail you? When your back is against the wall and you're out of ammunition, then what do you do?"

Bailey shrugged.

"No answer? Well that just won't do when you've got a son of a bitch trying to rip your head off!"

He turned to Babacan who seemed to have enjoyed himself.

"You know Jafar fought beside me for many years?"

Babacan nodded.

"One of you big bastards can be a big help in a tight spot. I hear Jafar is busy ruling the empire I gave to him, but there is still room on my team. Want to fill those shoes?"

"It would be an honour."

Taylor could see the Humans beside him were less than impressed, but they were powerless to act.

Good luck bullying him, Taylor thought, smiling at the prospect.

"Lieutenant?" Taylor asked.

"Yes, Sir?"

"You have been given access to a whole world of resources for this team, and we can have anything we want, is that right?"

"I have been ordered to give you anything you need, and those orders come from the President and Lord Jafar. Not even General Fin can block our activities. What is it you need?"

"Time we sorted out the deficiencies in our equipment."

"We already have the best gear there is," he replied.

"Best at what? Is it the lightest? Best protected? Best camouflaged?"

Jones shrugged.

"You're geared up for the wrong war. Now, first things first, we used to use exoskeleton suits that increased our strength and load bearing capacities several times over. If we're gonna stand a chance when we take on whatever it is you encountered, we are gonna need something similar."

"We just don't use anything like that for combat personnel."

"Yeah, well who does?"

"Maintenance crews, engineers, that kind of thing."

"Show me."

* * *

Taylor and his unit stood before a vast hangar nestled away in a part of the base that looked almost abandoned. He punched in a code on the keypad entry system, and two doors ten metres high slid open. Vast racking systems ran the length of the half kilometre-long structure, and they were filled with equipment, light vehicles, and machinery. Thick dust lay over much of what they could see.

"What is this? The junkyard?"

"Pretty much, Sir," Jones answered, "Apparently, this is where obsolete and unused kit gets stored."

"As I said, junkyard."

"Not a lot of heavy lift suits still in use. Most of the work has been taken over by robotics and remote control droids. No point putting a guy in a suit when that guy can control a robot. Stay out of danger, and it makes life a whole lot easier."

"Right up until the point where you need a man to do the job, and a machine just won't do."

"Why such hostility towards our technology? I thought a fighting man like you would relish the ability to save the lives of those under his command."

"I never send men or women to their deaths. I send them to do a job right, and sometimes they die. That's the price of war. You honestly think a remote control soldier can be a replacement for having boots on the ground?"

"I do."

"Yeah, well we'll see about that."

Taylor stepped inside and immediately caught sight of the heavy lift suits Jones had been talking about. They were a little bulkier than the Reitech exoskeleton suits he was familiar with, and they had no armour or weaponry at all. The suit covered much of the body, but in an open skeleton style structure to protect against heavy objects, not ballistics or blades. At the hands were huge hydraulic pincers. Taylor stepped up and climbed into one of the nearest suits.

"Whoa, Colonel, what are you doing? You are not rated to use one of those."

But Taylor ignored the Lieutenant. He stepped into the suit, and it immediately clamped shut around his body and powered up. He jumped out of the storage rack and landed amongst some of his unit who back away in alarm. The suit wasn't horrendously bulky and only increased his physical size by thirty percent.

"Colonel, you must be trained and qualified to use a heavy lift suit. I must insist that you power down and get out," said Jones calmly.

Taylor ignored him as he lifted his hands and looked at the pincers he now controlled. He took a few paces over to where one of the hover vehicles rested in a state of disrepair. He reached down, clamped the grips onto the lower framework, and lifted it with ease.

"Oh, yeah, this'll work," he stated with a smile.

"Colonel..." Jones went on.

"Quit your bitching, Lieutenant. You're a soldier, not a traffic warden. Draw thirty of these suits and have them armoured up. They just got reclassified."

Jones was shaking his head.

"It's not as simple as just pick and choose equipment,

and then have it entirely customised for an entirely new purpose."

"Damn right it is. Suit's pretty good as is. Send them to whoever does the maintenance on them, and have them liaise with vehicle repair crews. Shouldn't be too hard to get some armour welded on. It'll give us at least fifty percent coverage. The load bearing capacity of this suit has to be pretty high, so make use of it, armour it up."

"I'll have to clear this with my superiors. It could take some time."

"Do what you gotta do, Lieutenant. But have these suits armoured up and ready to serve in seventy-two hours."

"We can't..." Jones began, but Taylor interrupted.

"Can't!" Taylor yelled, "Hell I don't want to hear that word out of any of your mouths, ever. We can, and we will. Now you improvise, and make this happen. We adapt to overcome all adversity, you got that?"

Jones begrudgingly agreed.

"Next thing. Your report said that even when using AP rounds, the issue rifle you used was having a hard time against...whatever they are you were fighting."

Jones felt a little sick and went white as he thought back to the harrowing experience and nodded in agreement.

"All right, so we've sorted out strength issue, time to get the big guns out. Time to hit the armoury. Lead the way."

"Sir? If I may?" asked one of the men in his unit in a thick Scots accent.

"Yes...Private?"

"Murray. Sir, it seems like you're rewriting the book on everything we ever learned. Would it not be wise to use the skills and equipment we have that have been refined over, well, the hundreds of years since you have been away? Things have changed."

"Yes they have, and you know what? Not all change is good. You've grown soft without any real threat in your lives. You think because you're a professional soldier that you know what war is like. You don't, but you will, and if you want to survive it, you'll listen. I have in my time acquired a great many skills and a whole world of knowledge that has made me what I am today. All I am is a fighter, a marine, a weapon. That is what each and every one of you must become, the perfect weapon. Since such a thing doesn't exist, I intend to push you to the limits in pursuit of that goal."

He knew it sounded bleak, but that is how he thought now. He was pleased to at least have a purpose in this new life.

* * *

Taylor stood with his arms crossed and looked at a rack of weapons. Jones and Babacan stood either side of him. He was shaking his head he looked from one to another, and Jones waited for the next ridicule of what they had. Eventually, Taylor picked up the largest weapon there, the standard K15a that every soldier and marine used. He slammed in a magazine and took it to the end of the room where there was a firing range and fired a few shots. He didn't look impressed.

"The K15a is an ultimate evolution of the assault rifle," stated Jones, "Its lineage can be taken right back to the Reitech rifles you used to use, but not with a smaller calibre bullet and caseless ammunition. Same penetration, but substantially increased ammunition capacity and reduced weight."

"So you made it easier to use, great," Taylor replied sarcastically.

"So that was good enough for your days, but not ours?"

"Guns get bigger and more powerful as time goes by, Lieutenant. Those who stay the same lose the arms race. If your reports are right, then we need something bigger. What do you do for support weapons?"

"Support?"

"You know, when you need to put down some real firepower. Suppressive fire, bunker busting, anti-armour, all the big stuff."

"None of that is man-portable. We have armoured vehicles to do that sort of work."

"They did you a lot of good fighting in the confines of a star ship, didn't they?"

Jones could see his point.

"All right, so let's take this to the next level. We have to go big. Let's see the vehicle-mounted weapons."

They carried on through the armouries until the room opened up into a vast open plan area where maintenance and work was being carried out on several vehicles. The first thing that caught Taylor's eye was a turret with a massive gun barrel. It would serve him no purpose now, but he could see him coming back to it soon enough. But his attention was soon drawn to a smaller multi-barrelled weapon protruding from a cupola on the same turret.

"What is that, a Gatling?"

"Pretty much," replied Jones, "The Hydra. She fires a slightly larger round than our K15a, but at three thousand rounds a minute."

"There's a lot to be said for throwing more lead at the enemy. Let's take a look at one."

Jones led the two of them over to a counter where two of the weapons were laid out.

"Ah, now we're getting somewhere."

He leaned over and took hold of the vast multi-barrelled weapon and tried to lift it. He got just the lighter end of the top as he strained to manage the weight before giving up.

"Babacan, pick that up for me."

The alien obliged and hauled it off the counter, though it was clear that even he struggled a little.

"Think we can use that with the heavy lift suits?"

"Yes," he replied bluntly.

"Right then, we'll take a couple. What else is there kicking about around here?"

Jones pointed to a single barrel weapon with a large square head shield. It was almost two metres in length.

"We fit these on recon and scout vehicles as well as some light fighters, single fire only. The barrels can't take the heat build up for anything suppressive. Five times the armour penetration of our K15a, they're limited to sixty rounds a minute maximum, but they hit hard."

"Sounds like a good battle rifle."

"If you're hunting big game," replied Jones.

"Trust me, we will be. Think you can get the length down below a metre and a half?"

"There were such modifications tried a few years ago. Accuracy suffered over two hundred metres, so the plan was dropped."

"Yeah, well I guess you never dreamed they'd become our new infantry rifle. Get them modified and ready to go."

Jones nodded in acknowledgement.

"That all?"

"No. Something we learned early on, never underestimate the enemy, and there is no such thing as overkill. What have you got that has some really hitting power? Something that will go through the toughest armoured vehicle in service?"

Jones looked at him in surprise.

"Only one thing that could come anywhere near to man portable."

"I'm listening."

Jones pointed to one of the small hover vehicles like he had travelled in before. This one had the front passenger seat removed, and a three metre-long gun barrel fitted in its place. It was almost as long as the vehicle itself. Taylor knew nothing about it, but he didn't need to.

"We'll take one."

"Colonel Taylor," a voice said beside him.

He turned to find General Fin, but he knew he had not been there a moment before. He knew it was a hologram, and he could just see some image distortion to tell for sure.

"Taylor, the time for preparation is over. We have an operation departing in thirty-six hours, and we want you on it. Gather your team and be ready to depart in the next twenty-four hours."

The hologram of the General vanished before he was able to could speak a word.

"Twenty-four hours? We can't have all this kit ready by then. We'll just have to go with what we've got."

"There's that word again, can't. I don't want to hear it,

Jones."

"But this is insane, one day preparation?"

"War doesn't wait for any man."

"It's still not enough time to implement all this equipment and the changes."

"Then we'll do the best we can. The suits are working. Remove or retract the pincers so we can use these weapons. Just do what you can in the time we have."

CHAPTER SIX

The doors to the assembly room slid open, and Taylor stepped out in the lead of his unit. A shuttle was waiting for them just fifty metres away. General Fin and five of his staff were waiting to see them off, but their faces were in utter shock as their eyes looked back and forth across the line. There were twenty-four fighters striding towards them. Every single one wore a modified heavy lift suit. All they had done was weld on two plates to the torso area for protection and painted them green. They carried the vast vehicle-mounted weapons that Taylor had selected and were an alarming sight.

"Is all of this really necessary?" Fin asked as they reached him.

"When what you're doing isn't working, you do something different."

"Fair point," he replied, still looking at their hardware in amazement.

"Taylor, I am placing you aboard the Guam. She's a fine ship and the Lieutenant here is already familiar with her crew."

"What's the mission?"

"You're heading into Cholan space. They've lost contact with two stations and two colonies. All reports so far would suggest those areas have been devastated. This new threat is spreading like a scourge, and it is the Cholan people who are bearing the brunt of it. We need to stem this flow before it gets any further. I know you fought for Earth, but you must understand that there is a lot more at stake here. You are not fighting for one race and one planet, but all of the Allied races and their worlds."

Taylor brushed off the General's attempt at a rallying speech.

"What's different this time?"

The General looked confused, so Taylor continued.

"This is the second time you've made contact with this new race, and both times they kicked the shit out of you. What has changed? What are you doing differently?"

Jones looked horrified by the way he spoke, but the General held up his hand to stop him before spoke.

"It's okay. I understand your reservations, Colonel. I have studied your file, or as much as I could. You've got a colourful history to say the least. I will be honest with you; a lot of high-ranking members of the Alliance think bringing you back was a waste of time and resources, and merely a pipe dream of the only two friends you had that are alive today."

"More words, they are useless. I need facts. Please cut the bullshit and answer the question."

The General sighed, but finally he obliged.

"The Aranui are sending six vessels on this mission. The Human fleet will be three times what was sent to

Kepler. The Cholan Empire is amassing everything they can to rendezvous with you."

"And the Krys?"

"Lord Jafar is travelling to Tau Ceti to attempt to rally many of the independent factions there. In the meantime, he has sent his most senior and trusted servant, Sarik, to lead the Krys element of this venture, which is no small quantity of vessels. The fleet that was sent to Kepler was substantial, but only when we knew the true extent of this danger did we get the complete backing of Alliance leaders."

"Politics, it's all crap," replied Taylor, "A threat existed and you poked it with a stick. That is no way to wage a war. You see something dangerous; you hammer it dead with everything you got. How many times do I have to say it? There is no such thing as overkill. So answer me this, General, have we really got everything there is for this mission or not?"

Fin looked hesitant to answer.

"That's what I thought."

He stepped past the General without another word.

"You think we're being fed into the lion's mouth, don't you?" Jones asked.

"I don't think, I know."

"And yet still you go without fear?"

"I don't run wars. I just fight them. I'll work with what I've got."

Jones put his hand on Taylor's shoulder and stopped him when they reached the ramp to the shuttle.

"I get there's nothing left for you here, and you might be okay with this as a suicide mission because of some crazy death wish, but don't take us along for the ride."

"Is that what you think about me?"

"I do. I don't think you can accept this new existence. That you'd rather just go down fighting as you thought you did all that time ago, and who cares who suffers with you?"

"Then you don't know me at all, and your ancestor, my dearest friend, would be rolling in his grave. How dare you question my motivations? I gave up everything to save this existence that you now have, and one more thing; I never lead men to their deaths, not even the ones I despise."

Taylor turned and went on, leaving Jones speechless. They did not say another word to each other on the route to the Guam. When they landed aboard the vessel they found there was just a single officer there to greet them, a young female Ensign who looked unsure of how to act towards them.

"Welcome aboard, Sir," she said hesitantly.

There was no pomp and ceremony, and Taylor didn't mind that, but he could already see that he wasn't being made welcome.

"I am to show you to your quarters, Colonel," said the young woman.

Taylor nodded in agreement and followed on. He didn't even ask her name. He was more interested in the ship, but she noticed him studying it as they continued.

"Impressive, isn't she, Sir?"

Taylor grunted.

"The Guam is one of the finest ships ever made. She's fast, strong, has the best shielding system of any Human vessel twice her size. She has fifty fighter bays and the most advanced weapon systems on offer today."

"Is that supposed to impress me?"

"I hope so, Colonel. She will carry you to safety and back."

"I think that's actually our job."

The Ensign looked confused so she kept silent. Taylor was still looking at every element of the ship as he made his way through. To him it just looked like a smarter version of so many more he had served on before. It didn't look like a warship, but a civilian transport to his eyes. There were relaxation areas on every floor and every fifty metres. Lavish decor and lighting created an unnecessary ambience that seemed entirely at odds with the vessel's purpose.

But worst of all for him was to see the faces of the crew. They were fresh and naive. A world apart from the war weary men and women he used to see every day. It wasn't that he wished it on these people; just that he knew their world was about to be rocked.

"This is the ship you went to Kepler-186 on, right?" Taylor asked Jones.

"For the second time, yes. The first vessel is still undergoing extensive repairs."

"So the crew here have some combat experience?"

Jones shook his head.

"No, Sir. All wounded were removed to undergo recovery and recuperation. Most of the rest were put on leave to get over the tragedy they experienced. They were traumatised."

Taylor was already shaking his head in disbelief.

"So you threw away any combat experience we had and started from fresh?"

"That is the way the Navy operates. Each vessel had a minimum of two full crews working on rotation. It means everyone gets enough time of their own with their families, or wherever they want to be."

"That's great when there's no war to fight."

They stopped at an entrance to the accommodation that had been provided for them. It was a narrow corridor with a door every two metres. In each door was the tiniest of rooms, just large enough for a single adult to stand up or sleep on the bed that took up almost the entirety of the space.

"Luxury," Taylor stated.

"Everybody has the same space here, Colonel. From the mechanics to myself, even Commander Cohen."

Taylor sighed. He could see no one else aboard the vessel was eager to make him welcome, so he walked into the nearest room and hit the door switch behind him. He went to the corner by the bedside and powered down his suit, stepped out, and slumped down on the bed.

He could think of nothing now but Eli. The love of his life, and it occurred to him that he didn't even have a picture of her. He tapped the info icon in the pad on his forearm that was built into his suit.

"What can I do for you, Colonel?" asked the pre-programmed female voice of the machine.

"Find a photo for me. Sergeant Eleanor Parker. USMC, and Inter-Allied Regiment."

To his surprise a photo was suddenly projected before him. It was the photo from her base ID. He remembered it well. It was taken long before the first alien invasion began. He clicked to save it to memory. Next he turned his attention to the only other connection he could think of to the ones he loved. He brought up the messages from Coco and hit play before laying back to trying to forget the world until he could get to sleep.

* * *

Taylor woke abruptly as he dreamed of his fight with Erdogan. He felt the sharp impact of the enemy Lord's blade drive through his torso, and it almost felt real. He shot up out of bed and was dripping in sweat. But as he got to his feet, he realised all was okay. He hit the door release and stepped out of the painfully claustrophobic room that was more akin to cell. Taylor couldn't help but feel he had entered a life that had been cleansed and sanitised of all he knew and liked. He turned back, pulled on his combat uniform, and strode out looking for something to occupy his mind.

He wandered through the ship without recognising a single member aboard, and likewise he was invisible to them. He thought back to the fame he had achieved at the height of the wars. He smiled to himself as he thought of how oblivious they all were to who he was. Forgoing fame and all the attention that came with it was the first and only thing he liked about this new life. He never wanted fame, only to win.

He reached a huge wall of glass and could see dozens of the crew training with gym equipment inside. Some appeared to be practicing martial arts. On the far side of the room he spotted Jones. The Lieutenant was working through a form of solo drill or kata. His movements were impeccable, like a dancer. It made Taylor laugh to think of the rough brawler nature of Charlie Jones, the Lieutenant's ancestor.

Taylor could not help but step up to the automatic sliding door and enter. Everyone inside wore navy blue tight fitting shorts and t-shirts. They looked more like professional athletes training for sport than fighting men and women. He stood out in stark contrast to them all in his fatigues and combat boots. A few stared at him, and it was clear he was expected to dress as they were, but he didn't care. He stopped two metres short of Jones and watched him as he continued through his solo drill.

Jones weaved back and forth through a series of kicks and punches. He rotated and spun in a balletic fashion. Taylor was both impressed and appalled all at once, but it made him smile also.

"I thought you didn't ever need to fight with your own hands?" Taylor asked him.

Jones did not stop but answered as he continued to flow.

"We learn to control our bodies for our own quality of life, and to better ourselves as Human beings. We have no need of fist fights in this age."

As Jones went into a spin to begin three hundred and sixty degree kick, Taylor paced confidently forward and swung a punch that landed squarely on the Lieutenant's jaw. It sent him tumbling to the gym floor. He landed hard. To his surprise he put a finger to his mouth and realised blood was dripping from his cut gums. Everyone in the gym froze and watched in amazement and horror at Taylor's brutality, but none of them could lift a finger to do anything.

Jones was still in shock for a moment as the pain surged through his face, and he looked up to see Taylor looming over him in an ominous and unapologetic fashion.

"You don't think you need to fight with your hands, anymore? So what do you do when the other guy feels like giving it a shot?"

He looked up at the audience he had drawn and raised his voice for all to hear.

"Hey? What do you do? Do you run and hide? Lie down and die? It's time you all understood what it is we do. This isn't a pleasure cruise. You aren't here for fun. When someone or something comes to kill you, and you ain't got nothing left but your own two hands, you better know how to and be willing to use them. You don't hold back, you don't pussy out, and you don't tell me we don't need that! Fight, with everything you've got!"

His words cut into Jones who was now burning with anger, and that is just what Taylor wanted. The Lieutenant swept a kick for his leg while still on the floor, but Taylor just moved his lead leg back and gave ground. Jones rolled onto his feet and now stood before Taylor in a fighting stance.

"Finally found your balls?" Taylor asked. It almost sounded like a sneer.

"I've been training my entire life; where have you been all that time? On ice! You're old, weak. Nothing more than a brawler."

"At last, your true colours. You're going to eat those words soon enough."

Jones' face was going red with rage now, and he went forward with a quick kick towards Taylor's head. He was surprised by the speed and narrowly avoided the kick, but Jones spun into a second and clipped Taylor in the face. The impact snapped his head to the side slightly, and even Jones stopped in shock, but it didn't come close to shaking Taylor. He grabbed the stunned Jones by the throat and smashed an elbow into his face. Blood burst from the

Lieutenant's nose as he stumbled back.

But Taylor did not stop there. He went forward in an unrelenting manner. Jones could see he had to fight for his life now. He snapped a quick jab forward that only served to slow Taylor by a fraction of a second. He tried a powerful turn kick to his stomach, but the Colonel caught the leg, and Jones was locked. He tried to get free but Taylor held him with a vice-like grip, and with one big punch into Jones' face he was smashed to the ground. He writhed in pain for a moment and came close to unconsciousness, but as he opened his eyes, Taylor stood over him and offered out his hand. Jones was initially suspicious.

"Don't mistake my lessons for a desire to hurt you. All I want is for you to have the best fighting chance when it counts, and I need to know I can rely on you. Can I?"

Jones nodded slowly, accepted Taylor's hand, and was hauled to his feet.

"You know your ancestor, Charlie Jones. He gave his life to save us all, and I would do the same for you. Will you place that same faith in me?"

Jones was astonished, but agreed. He was in awe of how Taylor had handled the situation. He realised now that he had judged the situation entirely wrong. He opened his mouth and began to say sorry, but Taylor interrupted.

"No, none of that. We're comrades, not lovers. Now get that nose fixed up."

He smiled back at Taylor, and his teeth were red with blood. Taylor knew he had finally made a friend, and that he needed such an ally by his side. But as Jones turned to leave, an announcement came over an open channel in the room.

"All crew report to your stations."

"This it?" Jones asked.

"We have to be close now. Have the unit gear up, full kit. Be ready for anything."

* * *

Taylor strode onto the bridge in his new armour. Many of the crew looked at him as if he were some kind of monster.

"Colonel Taylor, please remember that you are here in an advisory role only. Our Marine contingent will handle any necessary tasks that may present themselves," said Commander Cohen.

Taylor had never met the woman, but he could already see he was getting the cold shoulder. He thought about responding sarcastically but knew it was a waste of time.

"How far out are we?"

"We are about to rendezvous with the Cholan grand fleet. From there will proceed to the last known location of the enemy."

"The screens in front suddenly zoomed forward to the Cholan ships in the distance. The vessels looked ungainly. The bows appeared bulbous, the engines too small to propel their substantial size. The fleet comprised of more than fifty warships, including twenty as large as the Guam, and a capitol ship five times her size. The vessel lay in the centre of the formation as a symbol of power, but to Taylor it just looked like a big juicy target.

"For small people they sure do build big ships, compensating for something there, you think?" Taylor asked with a smile, but none of the bridge crew appreciated it. Cohen scowled at him.

"The Cholans are our allies, and you would be wise to respect that fact."

"They're your allies. They are no friends of mine yet. I'll be the judge of that."

Many of the crew were startled at how Taylor talked to the Commander, and yet nobody would call him out on it.

"Sir, I am getting energy signature anomalies," said the one of the officers from their station.

Jones stepped up beside Taylor as the Commander responded.

"Where are they originating, and can you confirm they are a match?"

"That's the Nakbe. They say it is the most powerful ship in existence, even beyond Aranui technology," Jones said, pointing to the huge Cholan vessel.

"We can only hope," replied Taylor.

There was a brief silence as they were fixated on the scene before them. Several areas of empty space beside the Cholan fleet began to distort and glimmer, and Jones knew exactly what they were looking at.

"Ambush!" he yelled.

But even before anyone could say a word, the first shots burst out from three enemy vessels that appeared as if out of thin air. They were each the same vast mandible equipped ship.

"No..." said Jones in disbelief.

Taylor had no idea what he was looking at, but he could already see the power of what they were facing, just as Jones had experienced it. A beam of light burst out from each of the enemy vessels and obliterated two Cholan vessels in a single volley.

"One ship, there was only one before!"

"Shit happens," Taylor said quietly.

"Shield's up!" Cohen ordered, "Launch fighters!"

The familiar voice of Sarik came over the comms.

"All ships, engage the enemy," he ordered.

Nice subtle tactics, thought Taylor.

He watched the Cholan vessels open fire at their attackers. Missiles fired out from most of their vessels in huge salvos, and the Capitol ship was banking as if trying to bring some frontal weapon to bear.

"I hate this bit," Taylor said quietly to Jones, as the bridge erupted into a hive of activity.

"I thought you lived to fight?"

"This isn't fighting, not for us. We must just watch and wait."

"You know I never signed up expecting I'd have to fight anyone."

Taylor turned and saw the fear in the Lieutenant's eyes. He remembered that feeling. He remembered how gut wrenchingly horrible it was.

"Just keep breathing," said Taylor sympathetically.

He turned back to the battle to see that it was a full on brawl now. It looked like a bizarre version of nineteenth century tall ships duking it out with one another. The enemy battleship-like vessels had now been joined by twelve vessels one-third their size. They resembled a legless scorpion in shape and looked as ugly as they did ominous. Their pincer-like structures lit up with rapid fire pulse weapons that smashed into the Cholan fleet.

"In range in thirty seconds!" Captain Nichols shouted.

The Aranui vessels opened fire a second later. All of their beam weapons were focussed on one of the smaller enemy escort vessels. With their combined fire, they punched holes through the hull in two places, and yet still the ship continued to fire on the Cholans.

"Target the nearest vessel and open fire when ready!" Cohen ordered.

Just a few seconds later every weapon on the ship opened fire, and they could see the fighters closing in under their firing solution. Enemy fighters began pouring out from the large vessels to counter them. Another three Cholan vessels were blown apart before their eyes.

"How did you ever survive battles like this?" Jones asked.

Taylor shrugged.

"Half luck."

The Nakbe had a direct line up to one of the enemy capitol ships. The entire vessel seemed to glow neon green and finally burst with light as a massive beam burst out from its front. It must have been fifty metres wide and was almost blindingly bright. The beam of green energy struck one of the Morohta capitol ships head on and burrowed deep into the hull. Two of the mandible-like structures were blown off and holes erupted all over the right flank of the vessel.

Suddenly, the beam of light vanished, and they could see fires burning bright within the enemy ship. Without hesitation, the Commander pointed to the same vessel and shouted, "Target all weapons on that ship and bring her down!"

All fire focused on the crippled enemy vessel. Two-dozen other ships joined in to smash the enemy vessel for good. After almost a minute of bombardment, the engines failed and all lighting went out inside the crippled hulk. But even as cheers rang out on the bridge, they could see both of the other Morohta battleships turn on the Nakbe. The first pulse ripped into the hull, but one of the Cholan frigates blocked the path to the Nakbe for the second and took it full on. As the ship was blown apart, the rest of the Cholan fleet surged forward and closed the distance to create a wall between the Nakbe and the enemy battleships.

"We need to get in on this fight," Taylor said to Jones.

They were closing on the flank of the Cholan fleet now. They could barely see the enemy ships from the wall of gunfire and missiles that lit up the space between them, and Sarik's voice rung out once again to the fleet.

"We must protect the Nakbe. Do not let her fall!" he growled.

"How long does it take for that thing to reload, Jones?"

"I'm no expert on Cholan tech."

"Come on, you bored me with facts when you got here, what do you know?"

"They have often joked that it was such an immensely powerful weapon that it requires ten minutes to recharge, but it would never need to, because nothing would survive a single shot."

"Yeah, well I guess no one told these alien motherfuckers that."

The Nakbe was safe for a moment, but as Taylor looked back to the screen, he could see waves of Morohta small craft heading for the Cholan fleet. They were larger than the fighters that were already committed to the battle, and beside them were the torpedo-like breaching robots that Jones was all too familiar with.

"They're going to breach her!" Jones shouted.

"Target those craft. Do not let them get through!"

Cohen yelled.

The close range rapid fire weapons of the Guam opened up in a massive salvo, but to their horror many of the shots glanced off the enemy craft. Three were blown apart out of dozens. They continued to fire, but it was clear to all that there was no stopping them.

"Get me in there!"

"We haven't got time for your heroics, Colonel. Stay put and let the fleet handle this," ordered Cohen.

They watched as many of the craft came to an abrupt halt and latched onto the hull of the Nakbe while the breaching robots passed right though just as Jones had experienced.

"Can they hold off?"

The Lieutenant shook his head.

"Cholans have some big guns, but they have no chance in close proximity. They don't even have the equipment for it."

"Then come with me, Lieutenant," said Taylor as he turned and strode for the door.

"I gave you an order!" Cohen hollered.

Taylor stopped for just a second and looked back at the Commander.

"I don't answer to you. Fight your battle, Commander, and I will fight mine."

Cohen looked to others aboard the bridge to stop him, but nobody would dare. Taylor quickly turned and rushed out at a jogging pace.

"What's the quickest way we can get there?"

"A Sky King could have us there in less than a minute, but without really any protection or weaponry."

"Then get us one, now!"

Taylor raised his hand to speak on his comms as he ran. They reached the landing bays in under a minute, and the team was already assembled, but they looked terrified. Taylor did not break stride.

"On board, now!"

The Sky King had a long fuselage and bulbous cockpit at the front. The four engines looks unusually large and out of proportion for the size of craft. Taylor had never been keen on speed over armour, but needs must. They jumped aboard and found a solitary female pilot at the controls with no co-pilot.

"Get us moving now!" Taylor ordered as the ramp slid shut.

She looked hesitant for just a moment, but then went right back to the controls. They lifted off and soared out from the bays of the Guam, accelerating at remarkable speed. Beams of light and missiles flashed all around, and both Taylor and the pilot knew they couldn't survive any impact from the heavy ordnance that was being thrown about.

"What's your name, Lieutenant?"

"Alita Hariz," she replied quickly.

Taylor was surprised at her informality, and she spoke with a thick Scandinavian accent. Her helmet could not contain or conceal her bright blond hair and blue eyes.

"You didn't hesitate to step into this shit, why?"

"I've been waiting for this excitement in my life since the day I was born," she smiled at him.

Taylor laughed, as it reminded him of Eddie Rains, the pilot who had safely carried him through hundreds of death defying missions.

"You'll do just fine."

Taylor turned back to the view, and they were coming up fast on the Nakbe now. It was a vast vessel. Taylor knew he should be scared; he'd been here many times before, but somehow this time he was more excited than anything else. To him it just felt like a few days ago that he was locked in combat with Erdogan. He'd wanted nothing more than see an end to that war, but now he had nothing and nobody to live in peace with. This was all he had.

They were heading for the starboard fighter bays that he could see was shielded by shots impacting on the invisible surface.

"You get through that?"

"I've already sent confirmation codes."

"And if we aren't accepted?"

"We impact on the surface, and we'll be wiped out," she replied calmly.

Taylor just watched as they made their final approach, and to his relief, they passed through without any resistance at all. She brought them in on a rapid landing that caused them to skid to a halt. He turned back to his unit and found every one of them except Babacan looked white with terror. They needed more words than Taylor had time to give. He rushed up to the door and put his hand ready on the open button.

"You aren't gonna die here today because I won't let you. There is too much work to be done in this life for any of you to be quitting on it now. Let's move!"

His fist smashed into the button, and the ramp dropped down to the floor of the landing bay.

CHAPTER SEVEN

They hit the deck running. The interior of the Cholan vessel was like nothing Taylor had seen before. It was lavishly decorated in garish materials as far as the eye could see. The walls look more like the archways of an ancient monastery. Twenty metres away, crews were working to repair two fighters and were oblivious to their presence.

Taylor looked for the first entrance to take them further inside the vessel and soon spotted one.

"You've fought them before. What do you think their plan is?"

"They can't be worried about us escaping right now. They must be trying to disable the primary weapon, maybe even take control of it."

"Yep, that's what I'd do."

He rushed on into a corridor that was less than half a metre above their heads, and Babacan had to duck.

"Damn they are small," Taylor said, almost smiling.

Within a few paces, they could hear the sound of gunfire echoing through the hallway, and Taylor headed right for it. The corridor was opening out now into a more grandiose structure once more. They took a turn to find three humanoid-shaped robotic warriors stomping down a corridor while firing from weapons mounted in place of forearms. They were cutting down Cholan fighters who were incapable of standing against such relentless power and aggression, but they had their backs to Taylor's unit. He raised his new rifle and took aim.

"Sure hope this has got the guts for the job now."

He squeezed the trigger and watched the single shot hit the back of the nearest robot, jolting it forward like it had taken a heavy blow. One of the gun arms went limp, but the Mech soon began to turn to oppose them.

"Hit it!" Taylor yelled.

Four others joined him, and on a volley of fire the Mech was riddled with holes and collapsed to the deck. The other two turned their attention to the threat they posed, but Taylor did not duck for cover. He ran right at them. As he did, he activated his shield and held it out before him to cover his advance. He didn't feel at all confident of an almost entirely translucent shield made of some kind of projected energy, but it was too late now, he was moving entirely on instinct. He kept firing as he ran, but the shots were having less effect against the thicker front armour. The robotic soldiers reminded him of the hulking Mech warriors he used to face so often. They moved in a clumsy and slow way, but were a formidable and strong soldier.

Taylor lowered his rifle a little and shot at the knee joint of one of the robots, and the leg went out from under it. Its gun fired in an uncontrolled arc until it was shooting the other Mech beside it. It was all the opening and opportunity Taylor needed. He kept firing as he ran and finally smashed his way into the one that was on one knee on the floor, using all the weight and power of his suit.

While it was flat on the deck, he jammed the barrel of his rifle into the flank of the other and fired three shots until it dropped down. The other Mech raised its one good weapon arm to shoot at him, but he smashed it aside using his rifle like a club. Even as the Mech tried to get up, he put his foot on its chest and forced it down to the ground, putting his gun to its head and double tapping. All was then silent; only the faint sound of gunfire and screams in the distance could be heard. He looked back at his team. They had not moved from their original position and were frozen in amazement from what they had seen.

"Don't just stand there, come on!"

They reluctantly advanced. Only Babacan appeared to go forward with some enthusiasm. He was carrying the huge multi-barrelled Hydra cannon. They all froze as they heard a bizarre sound like dozens of hundreds of little feet pattering towards them. It was coming up from the corridor they were heading to. Taylor raised his rifle in readiness for whatever was going to come at them. It got louder and louder, and they knew whatever it was it was coming for them.

"Let's put that thing to the test," Taylor said to Babacan.

He nodded in approval, just as a swarm of what were almost robotic spiders rushed around the bend. They were on the floor, the walls, and the ceiling. Before Taylor could say a word, the swarm opened fire with a mass salvo of small arms fire. Dozens of shots bounced from his shield.

"Fire!" Taylor shouted.

Babacan pulled the trigger on the Hydra and the

corridor lit up. The rate of fire was so vast you could not hear one round from another. Thousands of rounds were thrown down the corridor. Taylor didn't even join in. He stood upright and marvelled at the devastation before him. It went on for almost twenty seconds until finally Babacan took his finger off the trigger. The gun barrels were red hot and smoking, and nothing was moving anymore.

"Fuck me," Jones said, gazing at the devastation.

It made Taylor smile to hear that Jones just couldn't contain himself.

"Thought you said all that vulgarity was all twenty-second century?"

Jones couldn't find any more words.

"Let's move," said Taylor.

They went forward and over the carnage that Babacan had created. Taylor felt the sound of one of the spider-like robots crunch and flatten beneath his foot as he landed squarely on it. All he could smell was burning metal and electrical component parts. They reached a crossroads and found three Cholan marines hurriedly approaching. At first they froze solid in terror, thinking Taylor and his team were the enemy, and yet didn't even bring their weapons to bear. They wore three-quarter length uniform jackets that looked more suitable for parade, with their ornate decoration and lack of any combat practicality. They wore no armour and seemed to carry no more than a handful of magazines between them.

"We're here to help," said Jones.

"Are they heading for the bridge?" Taylor asked.

One of them nodded.

"At the vessel's core. If they can access the power systems there, they will be able to destroy this ship."

"How do you mean?"

"The power generator for the primary weapon of the Nakbe is powerful beyond belief, and energy it generates must be contained, or it will destroy the entire ship. If they can release that power, we are all dead."

"That's just fucking great," said Taylor, "Design a wonder weapon that has a good chance of blowing you to high hell."

"The Nakbe is the finest piece of..."

"All right, I get it, shut the fuck up," interrupted Taylor. They were silenced by his imposing and rude manner.

"We're here to make sure something like that does not happen. Can you lead us to this power source?"

They looked hesitant.

"Hey, if it goes, we're all dead you said, right?"

They nodded.

"Right, then you have as much a stake in this as anyone. Lead the way," he ordered.

They went onwards, and Jones looked at Taylor with dread.

"You know about this?" Taylor asked him.

Jones shook his head.

"No, but I guess they were always gonna try and find a way to destroy the ship. This is just the ultimate solution."

Seemingly out of nowhere, one of the four-legged Morohta warriors flew from a doorway towards Jones. He turned to try and get his rifle on target, but it leapt onto him and lifted up one of its legs to thrust down into his face, but before it had a chance, Antos jumped and tackled the creature. They went tumbling down the corridor, and as they came to a standstill, he used the power of his suit to drive an elbow into the lit core on the warrior's chest. It cracked. He smashed his hand through and took hold of the source of the light and yanked it out.

The Morohta warrior instantly went limp, and Antos stood back up with a glowing slimy ball of organic mass in his hand. It looked and smelt disgusting, but he was still smiling anyway. It made Taylor proud to see one of his own take such initiative.

"You're learning," said Taylor.

Jones got up and went right to Antos. He put his hand on his shoulder and nodded to say thank you, as he could not find any words.

"This must be their brain," said Rocha, "They're mechanical warriors driven by an organic brain. No wonder they are so resilient."

"And easily replaced," said Bailey.

"Come on, we survive this, and we'll have all the time we can want for to study these bastards," said Taylor.

They carried on at a quick pace and arrived at a large domed room with golden arches on four sides. At the entrance to one was a hastily assembled barricade made mostly from crates. The bodies of Cholan marines were sprawled out all over them.

"Guess we're on the right track."

He went right for the line and jumped over the barricade without hesitation. There were almost twenty Cholan dead scattered about the place. Some had been hit by high power ballistic weaponry, but others seemed to have been skewered in close combat. A head lay separated from one body, and a leg from another. It made most of them feel sick, but not Taylor. He didn't know them or care for them, and he'd acclimatising himself to death a long while back. Several stopped to check on the bodies.

"No time, keep moving. We don't stop this, then we're all dead anyway."

They rushed on for another minute when they came across more dead Cholans. Double the number they found before. There were a few spiders destroyed, but they appeared to have shown little resistance. A hundred metres ahead they could see two of the massive breaching robots like Jones had first encountered.

"What was it you have been calling those things?" Taylor asked.

"Stalkers."

Beside them were three of the humanoid-like robots they had encountered before. As they approached, they could see both were wielding some kind of huge hammer and began to strike against a blast door. On each impact the hammer surface sparked with light as if it was igniting and blowing holes in the doorway. A dozen of the four-legged warriors lay waiting beside them and had just spotted Taylor's approach. It was clear they were not expecting any kind of trouble.

"Here we go! Kill them all!" Taylor shouted.

He got to a sprinting pace with the others following close beside him. Babacan somehow managed to get the hulking weapon he was carrying online and pulled the trigger. It wasn't accurate, but the enemy were showered with gunfire. Taylor opened fire himself, and the others at the front of the charge joined him. He took just two shots on his shield on the way in. One of the Stalkers seemed to come right for him personally. It looked like a formable close combat monster, and Taylor only wished he had his Assegai, the small thrusting weapon that had seen him to victory in so many battles.

Taylor fired repeated shots at the Stalker as he closed, and as they met, he jumped off his feet and threw his weight high at it. He struck it hard and rolled over the top, landing beside one of the hammer wielding robots. It took a clumsy swing for him. He ducked under and came up with a full view of its back. He fired three shots until his magazine was empty. The Mech was badly damaged but still moving. He smashed his foot down onto its arm and took hold of the hammer, prizing it from the Mech's grasp. He raised it above his head and smashed it down against the creature. Sparks flew, and it was like a grenade going off, blowing a hole in the torso of the Mech warrior.

Taylor couldn't help but smile at the weapon's effect. He now felt comfortable that he had something in hand to do a little damage. He turned to see the Stalker he had rolled over now had Bailey pinned to a wall, and she was straining to try and get free. Rocha lay wounded beside her with a puncture wound in her shoulder. Taylor jumped forward with his newly acquired hammer and swung it in a full rotation, smashing it down onto the top of the Stalker's body. The impact charge blew a hole in its body, and yet still it turned to face him, but in doing so released Bailey.

Taylor didn't give it a moment to gain speed for an attack, and he swung the hammer into one of its legs at the joint. The impact blew the leg clean off, and the Stalker staggered a little. Taylor immediately went forward with another swing at its other front leg, blowing it off so that it dropped face first to the floor. Lastly, he smashed it down onto the creature's head. The explosion burst the head apart and sent thick dark red blood spewing out in all directions, as the hammer passed through and smashed into the ground. He looked over to see his own people gunning down the other Stalker with shear weight of fire. There was nothing left standing. Another one of theirs lay wounded, and Antos had a deep slash across his face from one cheek right over to the other.

"That might actually improve you're looks," Taylor jested.

He could see they were all relieved, but more than anything, they had found the confidence that had been so lacking. However, it had gone a lost easier than Taylor expected, and that made him suspicious. Even as he was still thinking of what could come next, they heard the drone of enemy reinforcements approaching. He looked around for some cover to get them out of line of sight. Just off to one side was a two metre-wide opening that appeared to go on for some way.

The first of the enemy forces could be seen in the distance now, in the same direction they had come from. There were dozens of warriors and Stalkers.

"We need to channel their numbers. Get in there!" he said, pointing to the opening.

Gunfire hit their position as they rushed for cover. Taylor himself grabbed Rocha by the collar of her suit and hauled her across the deck. She cried out in pain. He got almost twenty metres down the corridor and pulled her up against a bulkhead so that she had a little cover and was sitting up towards the enemy. Nobody had gotten time to attend to her wound. Her uniform was bloody, and she was in real pain.

"No time for pain, suck it up," Taylor said, thrusting her rifle into her hands, "You want to live through this? Keep doing your job."

She put on a brave face and nodded in agreement. He stood up and assessed their position. They were split each side of the corridor, using all the bulkheads and supports for cover. The AT gun was already setup and ready.

"Whatever happens, do not turn away, do not run. You die fighting, or you don't die at all, got it?"

No one responded; they knew they didn't need to. He looked across at each of their faces, and there was no fear in them now. They were calm and ready. The first Stalker rushed around the corner and was immediately hit by the AT gun. The shot punched a hole right through the torso. It dropped dead and slid across the floor as the rest of the enemy took the bend. Taylor didn't have to say a word. The hallways erupted into a hail of gunfire, everyone focusing fire on the narrow opening they were being bottlenecked into.

Taylor emptied a full magazine in no time at all and slammed in a second. The bodies of warriors were mounting up now and were slowing their progress, but Babacan's Hydra stopped. Taylor could see he was out of ammunition, and he knew the rest of them were going through it at a rapid rate.

He went through another two magazines until he ran dry. He threw down his rifle and picked up the huge hammer he had taken from one of the Mechs. It was almost as tall as he was, but the suit he was wearing allowed him to wield it as if it were nothing more than a wooden axe. He held it at the ready behind the cover of a bulkhead and waited for the moment that the ammunition ran dry.

He was cursing under his own breath at the lack of hand-to-hand weapons amongst them. Then the moment came when several ran dry, and the others were coming close. They got off just a few more seconds of fire when Taylor stepped out with his shield before him and the hammer in two hands. A shot hit the shield, and another one clipped the face of the hammer, but he went forward without hesitation.

He pulled the hammer back and cocked it read to strike with his shield still covering him, but as he was about to take the first strike, they heard a thunderous boom from out in the main corridor where they had come from. It sent a shockwave through the floor and made the enemy stop dead and turn back. They began running away from Taylor.

"What the hell was that?" Taylor asked, expecting one of them to know, but they looked just as confused as he was. He chased on after the enemy with his hammer still cocked at the ready. As he got to the doorway, he could see flashes of light rushing past and stopped for fear of getting caught in the crossfire. He crept to the edge and peered around just enough to get a glimpse of the carnage around the corner.

He saw what was left of the Morohta forces was being cut to shreds by a sustained and relentless assault. The gunfire came to a halt, and he stepped out to get a full view. As he did so, a Krys Lord in full armour took a few paces forward and smashed down a huge glaive into the last twitching Stalker.

It brought back scarred memories for Taylor, and he froze before the alien Lord. His grip tightened around his hammer as he thought back to his epic fight with Lord Erdogan. But as he did so, the helmet of the Krys Lord retracted to reveal Sarik. He looked distinguished and old, but still as formidable as ever, or even more so.

Taylor smiled; the familiar face was a relief. He had known Sarik just a few days before he was put into suspended animation, and yet the alien had proven a great friend and ally.

"Hell, you're supposed to be in charge of this damn fleet, what are you doing down here in the dirt?"

Sarik smiled in response.

"You once showed me that sometimes a great leader must stand at the front and lead by example," he replied.

Taylor walked up to him and shook his hand enthusiastically.

"You know how good it is to see a familiar face?"

"You have been away from us for too long, friend."

"Yeah, and you got old."

"There is life in me yet."

"What the hell are you doing here?"

"Same as you. This ship, this weapon, it must be protected."

Taylor nodded in agreement.

They heard a violent surge resonate through the walls, and Taylor looked around in all directions for the source.

"It is the weapon firing once again," said Sarik with a smile, "Maybe there is hope for us yet."

"What do we do now?" Taylor asked him.

"We withdraw. This is a battle we cannot win."

"No shit."

"We have done enough damage that I believe they will not pursue us for now, but you should return to the Guam. She has taken severe damage and is still trying to contain a breach. We can handle this."

He nodded in appreciation and called to his unit, "Let's move!"

They ran back to the fighter bays at a sprinting pace and were relieved to find their Sky King still awaiting them. Taylor stormed aboard.

"Get us in the air!" he shouted before they were even all aboard.

The engines fired up, and they were off the ground just as the ramp was closing.

"You stop them?" Hariz asked, spinning the craft around.

"We're still alive, aren't we?"

She put all power down, and they soared back out to space. It was a horrific sight to behold. The gunfire had been reduced to a fraction of what it was. So many wrecked hulks from every race floated in such density it was as if they were flying through an asteroid belt. Bodies littered the space, too.

"Is this what it's always like?"

"Honestly, I haven't seen it this rough in a long time. Later years of the wars I fought, we put out a lot more hurt than we took," replied Taylor.

Two enemy fighters zipped past in front of them and were soon followed by two Krys and a single Cholan fighter close on their tail.

"But you made it though all that?"

He could hear the fear in her voice now. She kept her cool and remained flying, but he could tell she wasn't all right.

He placed a hand on her shoulder. Her skin-tight compression suit uniform meant he could feel her neck, and for a moment it took him right back to Parker. She took a breath in relief, taking comfort in the security she felt with him there, but Taylor quickly removed it. He felt his thoughts were betraying Parker.

"She was great to you, wasn't she?"

"How would you know?"

"Because it takes a great love to burn a man's soul like that."

Taylor didn't know how to take it. It was as if she knew everything about him.

She took them in for as quick a landing as they had made previously, but to their horror, they could see a Morohta ship in one of the bays as they put down. Taylor looked over to see their crates of ammunition were still stacked up on the loading bay not far away. He turned back to the others who were now raring to go.

"Head straight for the ammo, and take everything you can carry. We stick together and sweep and clear, got that?" He looked back to Hariz. He couldn't just leave her behind.

"You're coming with us. You got a weapon?"

She drew out a pistol from her side, and it opened out into a compact carbine.

"Sexy, but it ain't gonna cut it against these fuckers. You stay back and stay safe, okay?"

She nodded in agreement, and he could not but help let their eyes meet. There was something about this woman that both interested and worried him all at once.

"Go!"

The ramp slid down, and they rushed out for the ammo. For a moment it seemed they were alone, but just as they got out into open ground, a Stalker stepped out from where it was lurking, as if waiting for them.

"Keep moving!" Taylor yelled and turned to confront it. Hariz stayed with him and took aim with her carbine.

She fired two bursts that were accurate and controlled, but they did nothing at all. The Stalker seemed to circle him a little as if weighing him up. He grew tired of that and raised his hammer to go for a strike, but a bolt of energy soared from the creature and hit the centre of his torso plate. He was thrown back to the floor, and the hammer slid from his grip. He was stunned.

He began to regain consciousness and heard the familiar sound of Hariz's carbine chattering away, as she continued to engage the enemy. He stumbled to get up and regain his senses, but he saw the Stalker rushing towards her. He picked up his hammer but didn't have time to move. He swung it around and launched it through the air. With a stroke of luck, it smashed into the side of the huge mechanical creature and sent it tumbling over onto its back.

He took a few uneasy paces and collapsed down next to it. It writhed about, trying to get back to its feet, though it was badly damaged. Taylor could see the clear plate protecting the organic matter of brain as they had seen in the warriors. He took hold of one of the Stalker's own pincers and smashed it down onto the surface until it cracked. Then he reached in and pulled out the brain as he had seen Antos do. As he smelt the disgusting aroma from it, he finally passed out and dropped lifelessly onto the carcass of the Stalker.

Taylor awoke to find himself flat on the deck looking up at Hariz's face. His vision was blurred, and for a moment his mind wanted to tell him it was Parker, but his eyes said otherwise.

"Are you okay?" she asked him.

Her voice was soft and comforting, and his vision was

focusing properly now. Jones stood there with the hammer he had procured. He was cut on the cheek and above his eye, but he was smiling.

"This is a good idea," he said, lifting the huge hammer.

"Yeah, well, don't get too used to it. You can find your own."

Taylor tried to get up, but he was still sore. He stopped on noticing Jones offer out his hand, just as he had done when they fought in the gymnasium. He took it gladly and was hauled to his feet. He nodded in appreciation, realising that Jones' perspective had changed entirely. For a moment Mitch could see his old friend, Charlie Jones, in the young man.

"What happened?"

"You've been out for almost half an hour. We've cleared the Guam. Looks like we made it out."

Taylor started walking.

"Where are you going? We need to get you to medical."

Taylor shook his head and carried on, Jones and Hariz chasing after him. He was aching in many places, but it felt good. It was a reminder of good times. The success and ecstasy he felt after victory. Though he was also aware that this was far from a glorious victory.

"Please, Colonel.." Hariz pleaded.

But he shook his head and didn't stop. He passed several Morohta bodies en route. Human blood was splattered across many places where casualties had been taken away. He reached the bridge to find two of his own unit standing guard at the entrance. He passed through and found Cohen slumped in her chair.

The Commander looked up at him; her expression was of utter despair.

"Many survive?" Taylor asked.

Cohen shook her head.

"Did the Nakbe get out?"

"Yes, but it is hard to see how it can do us any good."

"Bullshit," replied Taylor, "So we took a beating. We gave one, too. If you aren't willing to accept the losses to fight for our survival, then maybe you are the wrong woman for the job."

"And you think we can win this?"

"Always, and if you don't believe it, you don't deserve to be here."

Cohen was shaking her head and began to weep.

"You didn't answer the question," he added, "Do you really believe?"

"Always. I wasn't born to lose."

He looked back at Jones and Hariz who stood waiting for him.

"I need a pilot to join my team, permanently. You want the job?" he asked Hariz.

"Yes," she replied confidently.

She was beaming with enthusiasm. He couldn't understand where that was coming from, but he was going to run with it.

"You can't just poach my crew," replied Cohen.

Her voice was shaky, and Taylor only shook his head, but it was Jones who stepped up.

"Actually, Sir, I have the personal authorisation of the President of the Alliance to acquire any and all resources that the Colonel requires. Lieutenant Hariz is ours now."

There was no fight left in the Commander. Taylor didn't know whether to be glad Jones had grown some balls or depressed that Cohen had lost hers, but either way, he was glad to have Hariz on board.

CHAPTER EIGHT

"Please wait here," said one of the guards outside the conference room on Ares 4 where Jones had previously been hauled up before Alliance leaders. He hated having to return there, but this time he had Taylor leading him. They were both still wearing their crude armoured suits. They were unarmed but were still an imposing sight. The Colonel ignored the command he had been given.

"Stop! You can't go in there!" yelled the man who had tried once before.

He went for his sidearm, but Taylor simply put his hand on the centre of the man's torso and shoved him quickly. He flew back and bounced off the wall. The doors opened, and the two of them strode in with security hot on their tail. They went straight to the centre of the room, and Taylor could sense the guns pointing at his back now.

"Stand down!" a voice boomed.

Taylor turned around and looked for the source. It was Jafar. The security immediately stopped in their tracks.

"Get out!" Jafar roared.

The security went back with their tail between their legs.

"What is the meaning of this?" President Isaacs asked.

Taylor looked over to him and back to Jafar, without even looking at the name plaque projected over him.

"Who is this?"

But Isaacs answered, "I am the President of the Allied races. Who, Sir, are you?"

"This is Taylor," replied Jafar.

"Taylor? This is Taylor? The man we resurrected from the twenty-second century? He doesn't look like much."

"No, but you couldn't ask for a better fighter, and a better friend."

The alien strode across the room and wrapped both arms around Taylor in a bear-like hug. He was clearly in the later stages of his life. His blue skin had faded and become deeply wrinkled. And yet with his age seemed to have come growth. He now stood almost as imposing a figure as Erdogan once had.

"Could have brought me back at a better time, don't you think?" Taylor asked him.

"There could not have been a better time. This is what you were born for," said Jafar, as he let him go and returned to his position. It was then that Taylor noticed Irala standing beside Jafar. He didn't appear to have aged a day. Taylor lifted up his hand and gave a casual and friendly salute to the Aranui Councillor.

"What is it we can do for you?" Isaacs asked Taylor.

"You've got some psycho queen bitch roaming the galaxy, and I don't see a lot of work going on to stop her. Where are the fleets? Where are the armies?"

"The fleet that we sent into Cholan space was already the largest armada in a hundred years."

"And it wasn't enough. So where is the rest?"

"Colonel Taylor, I do not much like your tone. You may be a simple man from simple times, but I still do not believe it would have been acceptable to talk to your superiors in this fashion, even back then."

"Of course it fucking wasn't, but sometimes someone has to cut through the bullshit and say it how it is."

"Okay, Colonel. I will entertain this for a moment, but only because Lord Jafar has spoken so highly of you. Tell us, how it is."

Taylor shook his head but continued anyway.

"You are facing a vastly superior enemy. I know a thing or two about that. We took the biggest fleet out to face them, and I'd be willing to bet that what we took was only just a fraction of their strength. They are going to cut a path through this universe with no one able to stop them."

"And you have some idea on how to do things differently? Some great plan?"

"I've got an idea. It's almost a plan."

"Then please, enlighten us."

"Okay. You, we...whatever, we cannot stop this enemy. The Aranui have already told us how dangerous they were the last time they were encountered. I've seen the extent of the forces you can put together, and it ain't enough, in quality or quantity. Throw everything you can muster against them, and we'll still lose."

"So you are saying this is it? We have already lost."

"No," Taylor quickly replied, "I am telling you that we must do something differently. You have God knows how many worlds, access to resources, manpower. The only resource we do not have is time. With enough time, I believe we could build the fleets and armies needed to take this battle on, but right now, we're fucked."

"But how can we buy time?" asked Isaacs in amazement, "You have said yourself that we do not have the fighting capability."

"No, we don't. But you're thinking this all wrong. Every step of the way we have been on the defence here, always on the receiving end. It's time we struck a blow back that resonated through their race. Something that will stop them in their tracks, and give us the time we need."

"And how long do we need?"

"Six to nine months, I'd say."

Isaacs gasped.

"You're living in a dream. You want to attack a technologically superior enemy, and somehow think you can make a difference?"

"I didn't say I had all the answers, but I am telling you that if we do not bring this invasion to a standstill, I don't think any one of us will be here in a year's time."

Isaacs looked around the room for some comment. Nothing came, and he didn't expect it to, but then to everyone's surprise, Irala stepped forward.

"There may be a way," he stated calmly.

"Then spill it," replied Taylor.

The alien looked uneasy and unsure of whether to continue.

"Don't bullshit me now. You know I want only what is best for us all," said Taylor.

"If you know something that could make a difference, please do not withhold it from us," pleaded Isaacs.

Irala still looked very unsure. He looked to Jafar and then into Taylor's eyes.

"Please," said Taylor.

"Very well. But the information that I am about to disclose to you has kept my people safe for thousands of years. I tell you now only because I fear we may not survive this war either way."

Taylor shook his head, for he wasn't willing to accept that fact.

"You are all aware of the technology my people possess. We are able to jump ships and fleets throughout the galaxy without need of gateways. This is a technology that we have safeguarded to protect our existence. It was once stolen from us by the Lord Erdogan, and you must all be aware of how close that took us all to destruction."

Taylor nodded in agreement.

"But the Morohta also possess such technology."

"Then why do they not merely jump to our homeworlds and attack them directly?" Isaacs asked.

"Because Bolormaa is a cruel being. She revels in the suffering and angst of those she destroys. She will break each race down piece by piece."

"Back to the gateways, what about them?" Taylor asked.

"The secrets of their operation are hidden deep within our homeworld of Onesaka. You see no ship can navigate jumps through space without a navigation hub, an immensely powerful facility hidden in the core of our planet. Erdogan began to understand that, and for a while he came close to possessing full jump capacity, as we know it."

"So without it your ships cannot jump?"

"They have the capability, but not safely. No Captain would ever make a jump without access to the hub. It would likely be suicidal."

"Where are you going with this, Councillor?" Isaacs

intervened.

"The Morohta possess the very same technology. If you want to buy our Alliance time to prepare for this war, then destroying that hub is the only way."

Groans and sighs echoed around the room, and Isaacs simply laughed at the insanity of what was being suggested.

"Are you out of your mind, Councillor? You want us to send a fleet into enemy space, even if we knew where that was, and to attack their most carefully guarded facility? How can that ever be successful?"

The room went silent as everyone dwelled on their situation.

"How much time would it buy us?" Taylor finally asked.

"A Navigation gateway is extremely complex. If destroyed completely, it would take up to a year for us to replace. It is unlikely the Morohta could do it much quicker."

Taylor's eyes lit up with the prospect.

"But that does not change the fact that this is nothing but a dream," stated Isaacs, "We do not know where it is, and you have said yourself that we do not have the strength to face them and win."

"I didn't say we couldn't beat them in a fight," replied Taylor, "Just that we can't carry on the way we are going. With a concentrated effort, and with the element of surprise, I believe we could make this work."

"You're still just dreaming, Colonel. You know nothing about this hub."

"No, but I intend to find out. Use me. I am a weapon. Point me in the right direction, and let me raise hell."

He turned back to Irala.

"Can you find their hub?"

"It will be dangerous, but I believe so, yes."

They both looked to Isaacs for a decision. He slumped back in his chair and rested his head in his hands.

"I can't condone this," he said in a muffled voice, "We would have to commit resources that are needed to defend our colonies."

Even as he said it, a Cholan advisor rushed into the room and to their Ambassador. Everyone waited to hear the news, but they already knew what it was likely to be. The Cholan Ambassador looked sick to his stomach as he got to his feet with weak knees and spoke out with a shaky voice.

"The planet of Uxmal has fallen to the Morohta."

"Fallen? Completely?"

The Ambassador nodded to President Isaacs.

"One billion Cholans lived on that world. None of them had time to escape. The fleet in orbit was mostly destroyed. Only three vessels escaped to bring us this news. President, I am here on behalf of my people to ask you to do anything in your power to make this stop. We cannot survive this. And we have no doubt that when the Morohta scourge is finished with us, they will come for each and all of you. You must act now."

"We cannot send another fleet into Cholan space. We cannot afford such losses again. I am sorry," said Isaacs.

"Then you will let us die, one by one?"

"No!" Taylor shouted, "I will not."

He couldn't help but feel for the Cholan people, even though he still knew almost nothing about them. He thought back to Earth, and how heart wrenching to lose it once.

"You will not act without Alliance agreement, Colonel."

"Then don't force me to. This is our chance, probably the only one we will have, unless anyone in this room can think of something better. Give me access to what I need, and I will do everything in my power to succeed. Know that I never ask anyone to do what I would not. I will lead this. I will deliver the crushing blow with my own two hands if I need to."

"Is it not true that you have a death wish, Taylor? As has been reported by even your own second-in-command, Lieutenant Jones?"

Taylor looked around in surprise at the Lieutenant, and he could tell instantly that it was true.

"You said that?" he whispered.

For a moment he felt betrayal like a knife in the back.

"I believed it."

"And you still do?"

Jones shook his head and stepped past Taylor to address the President directly.

"Sir, when I wrote that report, I did not understand the Colonel. I did not agree with him being back, and I resented being attached to his team. But these past few days, I have seen changes in myself, and those who went with the Colonel, that I could never have imagined. I was wrong, and I am not ashamed to admit that."

"So you would follow Taylor on this mission, knowing the dangers?"

"I would, without a single hesitation. I know my history Mr President, and the one thing I know is that Taylor has achieved success in situations that you could never imagine another doing so, or even surviving the experience. Please put your trust in him, as I have learned to."

"What do you need to make this happen, Taylor?"

"As much as you can give me."

"And if you fail?"

"Then we lose this war, just as we are going to right now if we do not act."

Isaacs rubbed his head once more. It was clearly the biggest decision of his career, and they all knew they were gambling on a monumental level.

"Then you will have it," replied Isaacs solemnly.

"Thank you."

He turned quickly back to Irala.

"How long do you need to find the hub?"

"Maybe a day or two."

"A lot can happen in a day, a lot has."

Irala nodded and vanished as he stopped his hologram.

"I'll take the Guam. She has seen us through adversity once. Maybe she can take us to hell and back. But I'll need more. Jafar, what can you provide?"

"Five cruisers, and another five from Tau Ceti. They have committed themselves to whatever course of action I order. They are yours."

"If this device is buried deep in the core of a planet, then we are going to have to deliver some kind of device to it by hand. I've managed this before, and I will manage it again. I need access to the most powerful weapon you have got. No such thing as too powerful. If it's world ending, then all the better."

"We do not have such destructive weaponry. We have not needed them and banned their use and existence in the Alliance. We worked for better times, Colonel. Peaceful times."

"I get it. I fought my entire career for that. I just never got to reap the benefits, but now I need something. There must be a weapon, some kind of nuke? Something that can devastate this device."

"I am sorry, Colonel, I cannot help you. I do not have that kind of technology to give."

"I do," Jafar said.

Isaacs looked at him in shock and horror.

"How? There has long been an agreement about such weapons of war."

"Because I wasn't willing to risk a day like this. I will provide a bomb that will be sure to destroy the hub, and most life on the planet it occupies. Just do not be on that planet when it ignites."

"Okay."

"What else do you need?" Isaacs asked.

"Manpower. Your troops aren't geared up for this war. We've already begun to make changes, and I need these implemented on a much larger scale. Up armour, up guns, and I need access to weapons experts. People who can make this happen."

"Anything you want or need, if it can be provided, you will get it."

"I need someone go drive this along, make sure things happen."

"You have already met General Fin? I will ensure that he works to provide everything you need."

"What now?" Jones asked.

"We wait and hope. But right now I need a drink."

* * *

Taylor and his team sat at a bar on the space station. He looked at the full glass of ice-cold liquid before him. It was a bubbling light blue substance. He was told it was alcoholic and that was all that mattered. He licked his lips and raised his glass.

"To friends, comrades, and all those we have lost!" he shouted and raised his glass.

Many of them clashed their glasses together with him before throwing back the first mouthful and then slumping back down.

"You know this breaks all the regulations there are?"

"Really, Jones? I thought we were just having a drink after a hard fought day," he replied with a smile.

Jones pointed around the room.

"Look around, see any uniforms?"

Taylor shrugged. "Doesn't make any sense."

"No drinking allowed when active."

"Even off duty?"

Jones nodded.

"What kind of stupid fucking rule is that?"

"Regulations state that all personnel while on deployment must refrain from alcohol and all other controlled substances. They must be prepared and able for duty at all times of the day and night."

"Bullshit, that was written by an idiot with a stick up his ass."

"How do you mean?"

Taylor laughed. "Don't worry about it."

He took another sip and looked around at the happy smiling faces of his team as they chatted away.

"You see that?" Taylor pointed to them for Jones.

"I just see people enjoying themselves."

"It's priceless. Have all the discipline and rules you want, but if a group of fighters can't just chill out and make merry, you've got no hope of success in the field."

"So you think drinking makes you a better soldier?"

"Marine," he replied with a smile, "A better fighter, yes I do. Until this time you've never know war, right?"

Jones nodded.

"So you never knew pressure, the fear of death, of losing friends. You lived in a state of bliss with no real worries in the world."

"I wouldn't say, no worries."

"Trust me, you had no worries," Taylor replied firmly, "And when you have to put up with that shit, it will destroy you. It will break you down until your mind is gone, even if your body remains. Work hard, fight hard, and play hard."

"And when it's all over?"

Taylor took another sip and sighed. "I wouldn't know. I never really got to that part."

He threw back the last of his drink, but even as the glass landed on the table, a second fully loaded one was placed beside it. He looked to see Hariz had come to join him.

"Looked like you needed another," she said.

He nodded with appreciation as he took it. She shifted up the bench a little until her thigh and elbow were jammed against his. He wanted to move her away, but he was overwhelmed by how good it felt. Instead, he just lifted his glass and threw it back.

* * *

Ten hours had passed, and so far Taylor had heard nothing from Irala, and he was relying on Fin and Jafar to assemble what he needed. He stood in what looked like a laboratory, but was in fact an armoury and weapons development centre. He had completely phased out what the man before him was saying as he slipped into an endless drone. It was a level of technological knowledge and reasoning that he had no care for. He felt something tugging on his arm, and he snapped out of it. It was Jones trying to provoke a response.

"What's up?"

"What do you think?" Jones asked.

Taylor shrugged. He wasn't even sure what Jones was referring to.

"Assegai, tell me you have them?"

Jones shook his head and smiled as the technician in front of them continued.

"As I have already told you, Colonel. The Assegai, as you call it, is nothing more than an antique today. There are a few in museums and private collections, but we do not use them."

"Then make one."

"I could very easily. It is a crude and primitive weapon. Barely even a weapon really, but an imprecise cutting torch. I must insist that you consider the range of ballistic options we have on offer in this age."

Taylor stepped forward and right up into the man's face and well beyond his comfort zone.

"Got it, Doc, now get me. An alien bastard is this close to you. You have no ammo, you have no gun, what do you do?"

"But...but with the advancements in weaponry today, a situation such as you speak should never arise."

"Many things should never have happened. You can't predict life one hundred percent. I need the weapon for when everything goes to shit. The Morohta will rip you apart without hesitation. Make me something. You know what an Assegai is. Make it, same or better, and have twenty-two made for my team before we leave on our next mission."

"When is that?" he asked wearily.

"Could be in six hours, a day maybe."

"Colonel, I cannot work miracles."

"Yes you can. You just have to try a little harder."

Taylor lifted his hand, formed the shape of a gun, and pressed it to the side of the man's head.

"You ever been told that if you don't achieve something by a certain time, you will die?"

The man shook his head violently in fear at both the intimidation and imagery.

"Those are the sorts of deadlines we face. So don't tell me something can't be done. You do whatever you have to do, but you get me something that works."

The man nodded.

"What's your name?" Taylor then asked calmly and politely.

"Haines."

Taylor smiled. "Well, Haines, I have every faith in you. Good luck. Yeah...we're gonna get along just fine."

With that, he turned and left.

"That really necessary?" Jones asked as they stepped outside.

"Everyone needs a little motivation. Now he has found some."

"You sure do have a strange way of handling people. I thought you really hated people and had no respect for them. But now I am thinking this is how you show respect and friendship."

"Hey, there's plenty of stuff in this time that looks and sounds stupid to me, too."

Jones laughed.

"You know, this, the team, what do we call ourselves?"

Taylor shrugged.

"Honestly, I have no idea, but I leave it to you to come up with something."

Six hours later Taylor sat stripping his rifle and checking equipment with the rest of the team when the comms unit on his arm started to flash. He was waiting for news from Irala, so he quickly accepted, but to his surprise Haines was projected before him.

"Haines, what can I do for you? Have you worked any miracles?" he smiled.

"Yes...yes, Sir. I believe I have something that will satisfy your requirements."

"Then I'll be with you presently," he replied, abruptly ending the call.

"You see," he said to Jones, "You just have to find the right way to motivate people."

* * *

Taylor and Jones stood before Haines who held what appeared to be little more than a handle from a bike.

"I'm not sure you are quite getting this," said Taylor suspiciously.

Haines appeared to press a concealed button on the device, and it shot out to half a metre length, in what looked like a slightly longer Assegai. Taylor's eyes widened. Haines had his attention now. He turned around and thrust the weapon towards a plate of armour set up on a bench nearby. The tip flashed on impact and cut through like butter. Taylor was already nodded and smiling with appreciation.

"I am impressed."

"It is really very simple. I combined the elements of a shock baton and a cutting torch. What you now have is a retractable Assegai. Every bit as good as the antique weaponry you knew in your day, and now made better."

"You really came through," said Taylor.

He reached forward to take the weapon, but Haines interrupted.

"That is not all, Colonel," he said, pulling back the weapon from Taylor's reach, "Maintaining the shock baton's technology with the increased power source of the cutting torch, you may now use the edge to shock the enemy. It probably won't kill much, but it can deliver quite a blow, and also has the potential to destroy electrical components."

As he finished, he held up the Assegai and cut down with it against the metal plate. The edge connected, and it fizzled with energy and sparks erupted as it burnt into the surface of the armour.

"Not a relation of Reiter, are you?"

"The great Reiter?"

Taylor nodded.

"I could only wish. Reiter was one of the greatest of his generation."

"Yes, I know. He built me the first Assegai, and now you have filled his shoes."

Haines was glowing with excitement at the prospect.

"I'll be needing plenty more from you in the future.

Can you get more of these made quickly?"
　　"In small numbers, yes."
　　"Enough for my team?"
　　"Certainly."
　　"Then do it."
　　He turned back to Jones.
　　"It's time you all learned to fight the old way."

CHAPTER NINE

Taylor watched over his team as they slugged it out with one another in the gymnasium. They were in full combat gear and with shields up. But they used a simple wood training baton in place of the Assegai. He could see they were coming together now. Jones put down his baton and stepped over to Taylor to take a rest and get his breath back.

"This is positively medieval, you get that?"

Taylor nodded.

"Whoever told you war could be clean, they lied. But the Assegai is a great weapon. It will not fail you when you need it most. And I've been thinking about ammunition. With the extra armour we've been loading up on, I don't want to encumber the suits too much."

"Okay?" replied Jones.

"The drones you were so fond of, I want to use them."

"I thought you hated them?"

"I do, as fighters, but I'd be a fool to not see their practical application."

"Okay, what do you want to have me do?"

"I want a drone for every Human. They are to be unarmed. They can't shoot for shit, and I don't trust them in a combat situation. They are to be load bearers. They will carry ammunition and assist with the wounded."

"That could double, maybe even triple the ammo we can carry," replied Jones.

"Good, then get it done."

Before he could move, a hologram appeared before them. It was Irala.

At last, Taylor thought, but he quickly realised by the alien's expression that it was not good news.

"Come on, tell me you found it."

"No," he replied simply.

"What the fuck are we to do? You told me you could do this?" Taylor said desperately.

"There is still a way."

Taylor sighed. "And if you could do it yourself, you would have, right? So what do you need from me?"

"We must place a tracking device aboard one of the enemy vessels, and then we may track the hub from the moment it makes a jump."

Taylor shook his head.

"So you want us to bait one of those things in, and somehow survive the experience?"

Irala nodded.

"That's a pretty big fucking ask."

Irala simply nodded again.

"And there is no other way?" Jones joined in the conversation.

"No, I am sorry."

"So this tracker, can it be launched from a distance?"

Irala shook his head.

"I wish that were the case. The device is small, but it must be connected directly to the navigation and communication systems."

"So somebody has to go aboard and do this?

"We could send our Guardians, but..."

"But I'd rather have a man to know the job is done right," replied Taylor.

"Yes, I believed you might say such. Additionally, this is a tactic my people used once before to track the Morohta fleet. If the Aranui were involved, they may suspect and manage to jam the signal."

"Seems to be an awful lot of ifs and maybes here."

Taylor agreed with Jones.

"Crazy mission with little chance of success, just our kind of work," he stated, looking across at the team still training hard.

"Listen up!"

His voice carried to every corner, and they quickly stopped and listened.

"The Lieutenant asked me what we should call ourselves. We have no real identity, so what are we? I once led the greatest fighting unit in the galaxy. We were unstoppable. To most people we went by just one name. The Immortals. We would not be defeated, and our legacy would live on forever. I am here to tell you that the Immortals still live on, for they are you who stand before me today. I saw each and every one of you confront adversity and terror, and strike it down. You have earned the title. From this day forward, you are, we are, and always will be, the Immortals."

* * *

Taylor stood around a table with Jafar, Sarik, and the Admiral who commanded the Nakbe that was still being repaired at the station. Irala appeared before them, and Commander Cohen stepped inside soon after.

"This it?" Taylor asked.

They all nodded in agreement.

"Okay, you know the deal. We need to get this tracker aboard one of the Morohta battleships. I will do that, but I am going to need a lot of commitment to achieve it."

"Do you have a plan of how to make this work?"

"Yes. We split the fleet into three. I will take the Guam and a handful of other ships on what appears to be a patrol mission into Cholan space. I want to present a threat, but nothing too massive. Aim is to draw out a number of Morohta vessels, but not all of them. When they take the bait, I want the Nakbe and her support vessels to jump into Cholan space, some place a long way from us, but close enough that the enemy know you're there."

"Colonel, we cannot risk the loss of the Nakbe," pronounced the Cholan Admiral.

"Admiral Eme, I am well aware of the importance you put on that vessel. But I do not intend to place her in any more risk than is necessary. However, there is no way of doing this without some risk."

He looked very uncomfortable, but let Taylor go on.

"Most of the Morohta fleet should high tail it to your position, leaving just a small presence to take on the Guam and her fleet. I'd hope just one enemy battleship."

"Hope?" Jafar asked.

"We'll do everything we can to make this work, but at some point we are just gonna have to hope our luck holds."

"That is no way to wage a war or gamble with your resources," replied Eme.

"Tell me about it, and when you've got a better idea, you speak up," replied Taylor,

"Once the enemy fleet departs, we should be left with a small skirmish scenario. I intend to drop an EMP at close range, knock out everything on both sides, but not before I have reached the enemy battleship with a breaching team and the tracking device. If Irala will supply the Guam with EMP shielding, that will make our life a lot easier. At which point, the remaining third element of the fleet will jump in to assist us, forcing the enemy to retreat and jump."

"It's an ambitious plan, and a dangerous one," said Cohen.

"Can you see another way?"

"Maybe if we had time, but we don't. The Admiralty has left this one to us, or you more specifically."

"They just want a scapegoat if it all goes to shit."

Cohen shrugged, but it was clear that she knew it, too.

"All agreed?" Jafar asked.

Nobody said a word, so they took it as such.

* * *

Taylor stood aboard the bridge of the Guam once again. They were floating through Cholan space at a steady pace. Everyone aboard knew what they were walking into. They just didn't know when it was going to happen.

"You got those drones ready?" he asked Jones.

"Yes."

Taylor reached down to his Assegai to check it was there. It was a comfort to know he always had it on his person. The Commander got up and stepped over to him. She leaned in beside Taylor's shoulder so she could talk quietly.

"I'm sorry if I didn't trust in you," said Cohen.

"It's nothing new."

"How do you do it, though?"

Taylor squinted, trying to understand.

"Do what?"

"Keep surviving all this? No man should ever have been able to make it through all that you have. You defy the odds every single time you go into action."

"I've been almost killed more than a few times," he replied with a smile.

"Yes, almost dead, and yet here you stand, a relic who has taken command of the single most important operation of my lifetime. If someone had told me this is the way it was going to be just a few weeks ago, I would have laughed at them. You seem to be surrounded by some energy in the universe that wants you to live, and I am honoured to be a part of that."

"I don't believe in all that fate crap, you know that?"

"Maybe you should. Because logic and the odds would have you dead by now, today even."

Taylor agreed with her, though. He could never understand how he managed to survive through it all.

"We've got incoming," said Nichols.

They turned to see the jump signatures displayed before them.

"All right, here we go."

"Send the signal to Eme now!" Taylor ordered.

Nichols quickly got about it. "Done," he replied.

Four of the battleships appeared at close range with another ten frigate-size vessels.

"Oh, shit," said Taylor.

"Shields up!" yelled Cohen, "This better work. We can't take that on for long."

"Come on, take the bait," Taylor whispered.

Three of the ships flickered and with a flash they were gone, along with all but two of the frigates.

"It worked said," said Cohen in amazement.

Light began to flicker at the base of the mandibles of the Morohta battleship, and they all knew they might not survive an impact from its powerful weapon.

"Deploy EMP!" Cohen shouted.

The device soared out into view like a torpedo and ignited when it got to the halfway point. Everything went dark except for the Guam.

"How do they do it? EMP shielding, I've never seen it before," said Cohen.

"Yeah, Aranui like to keep a few secrets to themself. Can you handle it from here?"

Cohen nodded to Taylor.

"Like shooting fish in a barrel."

"Once they get comms back online, we could have a world of shit coming down on our heads."

"Then work fast," replied Cohen.

He looked over to Jones and nodded for him to follow. They got to a jogging pace and were soon rushed aboard the Sky King. The rest of their team were already there. Taylor didn't have to say a word as Hariz lifted them off the deck, and they soared out into space.

The first looming shadow of the huge battleship was a terrifying sight, but they watched the guns of the Guam smash the two smaller vessels relentlessly as they were unable to defend themselves. Taylor leaned in to the still empty co-pilot's seat to get a better view.

"About time they got what was coming to them," said Hariz.

"They'll get plenty more, but not today."

She moved her hand and rested it over his.

"Are you scared?"

He shook his head.

"There is too much at stake and too much for me to think about to be scared."

"But I am," she added as they soared towards the enemy battleship.

"Just focus, keep flying, and you'll be fine."

They covered the distance quickly, and Hariz brought them to a quick standstill, landing on the surface of the lower hull at what appeared to be some sort of access hatch. They felt the magnetic clamps lock onto the hull. Taylor pulled his hand out from Hariz's and went right to the door in the centre floor of the craft. Jones was already sliding it open.

Taylor felt no fear at all, just as he had said. He had been here so many times before. It was excitement he now felt. He lowered down a shaped charge against the ship and fired the trigger mechanism.

"We're in," he said.

He jumped down the small access corridor that had latched onto the enemy vessel and jumped inside. He landed on a floor that felt a little soft and organic, and looked around to see that much of the structure inside did indeed appear to be living. There were metal grated floors, and all of the supports and beams looked alive. Gravity was normal, and his console showed that oxygen levels were normal also. He hit the button on the side of his helmet, and the visor slid open.

To his amazement it didn't smell half as disgusting as he was expecting. It was like a light scent of sulphur and salt combined.

"Lead the way," Taylor said to Jones who was carefully studying the map given to them by Irala.

"If his people haven't encountered the Morohta in however many thousands of years, why do we presume the ship will be unchanged? You know how much Human life and design has changed in a thousand years."

Taylor nodded. "All too much," he replied.

"When you reach an evolutionary peak, there is no need to change. Irala said the Morohta were undefeatable. They stopped waging war because they wanted to."

"Wanted to? I doubt that."

"Agreed, but until we have an answer on that, we're just gonna have to make some assumptions."

"Assumptions are a cluster fuck. Stick to facts," replied Taylor.

"Yeah? Would if we had any. Why would an enemy that enjoys genocide so much just stop?"

Taylor shook his head. "I don't know, but I'd sure like to find out."

He looked down at his watch. They were down to ten minutes on the estimate of how long before the Morohta vessel regained power. The room they were in had pods on all sides. They seemed to be the equivalent of bunks, but they could not tell for what, and there was no sign of life.

"Come on, let's get this done," said Taylor.

Then when they thought they were all alone, a light flashed in the distance, and a pulse of energy soared towards them.

"Incoming!" Taylor hollered.

"They leapt for cover as they activated their shields. The impact landed just a metre from Taylor and launched him a little further than he had intended to leap. He landed hard and looked back to see the lifeless body of one of theirs. Their armour was smouldering from the heat of the impact, and Taylor could already tell they were dead.

Many were returning fire now and could see what was coming at them. It looked much like a Stalker, but with a large cannon-like weapon fitted on the top of its body. Taylor got to one knee and took aim, but he heard Jones' voice shouting behind him.

"Get down!"

He immediately dropped down flat towards Jones and looked back to see the AT gun barrel mounted on the Lieutenant's shoulder with the gunner standing behind him. They fired a single shot that rushed over Taylor's head and smashed into the creature. It hit at the torso near the base of its weapon, going a little higher than expected. The weapon system was blown off its back. Taylor jumped to his feet and let out a battle cry as he drew his Assegai and stormed towards the creature, which likewise did the same. As he closed the distance, one of the pincers thrust towards his face. He slid the shield under it, and that allowed him to smashed right into its body and drive the Assegai up to the hilt.

He drew the blade out and tried to stab again, but

one of the other legs came for him. He cut at it with the Assegai, and the blade flashed with light as it shocked the leg and caused it to drop momentarily. He used the opportunity to drive the Assegai home once again, and finally the monster went limp and dropped before him.

He looked back to his team. Jones was sitting over the body of the one they had lost, and the others looked on with horror.

"Come on, let's move!" he called to them.

He didn't like it any more than the rest of them, but they had a job to do. He reached the end of the room and found a corridor that either carried around the perimeter of the vessel, or another that went deep into the belly of the structure. He quickly headed inside. Jones was close behind him.

"Think they know we're here yet?"

"Doubt it, or we'd have been hit by a lot more," replied Taylor.

"It's so empty, why?"

"Looks to me like this ship is the size it is purely to power the ridiculous weaponry it carries. I doubt it needs an awful lot to crew it. Particularly if much of it is living material."

"Or it's a transport craft for armies we just haven't seen yet."

Taylor nodded in agreement and upped his pace. He knew they needed to progress slow and steady to be safe, but there was no time. There was a doorway up ahead, and as they reached it, one of the two-legged Mechs stepped inside. It spotted them and instantly raised its guns, but Jones and Taylor had already got off two shots each, and it was smashed back by the impacts. The guns on both of its arms began to fire, but the shots smashed into the floor as it took the beating, until finally it was finished and fell down into the metal floor behind it.

"This way," said Jones.

They weaved from room to room and corridors. They had little understanding of much of what they were looking at, and nobody cared at this stage.

"Do you really believe this tracking thing will work?" Jones asked quietly.

"If Irala says it will, it will," Taylor answered confidently. "We're almost there now."

The room opened out into a large dome. In the centre was what looked like the trunk of a tree. It was three metres wide and extended all the way to the ceiling, branching out to the corners of the room that was twenty metres wide.

"What on Earth is that?" Antos asked.

"It's what we're looking for." Jones showed a diagram to Taylor.

Taylor was relieved to have found it.

"All right, let's do this and get off this wretched monster."

Jones pulled the device from his back. It was nothing to look at, just a small box with nicely rounded corners. It appeared to be made from stainless steel, and yet was far lighter.

"What now?" Taylor asked.

"Irala said we just place it at the base of this thing."

"Then do it."

They were all sceptical, but Jones placed the box down at the base of the organic tree-like object and stood back up. For a moment nothing happened at all, and Taylor was about to curse his old friend when suddenly the box sprang into life. It seemed to prize apart in many different directions until forming into a corkscrew-like drill. It began to rotate and burrow into the base of the Morohta structure. In just five seconds it had entirely vanished inside, and the hole closed up around it.

"That what it was supposed to do, Jones?"

"That's pretty much what Irala said."

Taylor shrugged. It was bizarre, but he didn't care if it worked.

"Okay, then let's go. Last thing we want to do is give away the fact that we were in here."

Taylor rushed onwards to lead the way.

"That was anti-climactic," said Jones.

They reached the next corridor and stopped dead on finding six Morohta warriors blocking their path.

"You spoke too soon!"

Both sides opened fire simultaneously as they scattered to the walls for cover. The warriors were no match for the Immortals in their new found equipment, but Taylor couldn't help but wish for greater numbers. He leaned out from one of the organic support beams and took careful aim at a warrior. With a single shot, he hit the neck and blew the head off, killing it outright. He ducked back to cover and looked down at his watch.

"Fuck," he said to himself, realising they couldn't afford to get bogged down.

He could see Babacan stuck in cover and unable to get the Hydra to bear. Taylor held out his shield and rushed back to the Krys soldier's position. He held out his shield to cover Babacan's right flank.

"Antos!"

He yelled and gestured for him to do the same on the

other side. The two of them formed up around the alien and stepped out of cover with the huge multi-barrelled cannon between the shields. The second he was free of cover, Babacan pulled the trigger, and the room lit up as if on fire.

"Advance!" Taylor ordered.

They continued forward, giving cover to Babacan as he smashed the Morohta position and forced them down into cover. He killed two with the opening salvo, and Taylor watched as the others advanced now and joined the fight. Finally, the Hydra stopped, and two of the warriors jumped up to engage them but were hit by a volley of fire. Taylor rushed forward and jumped over two of the bodies, firing several shots as he leapt towards the last one and landed on top of it, as he continued to fire.

All went silent when a scream of his name rang out. He immediately recognised it as Rocha. He leapt up and turned just in time to see her fire several times at one of the hammer wielding Mechs that had come from a concealed entrance. Her shots did nothing. Taylor lifted his rifle, but there was no time. He could see almost in slow motion as the hammer swung towards Rocha. It smashed into her head and snapped her neck instantly. Her body was thrown like a ragdoll across the corridor and slumped lifelessly to the floor amongst the enemy dead.

Babacan spun the Hydra around and pulled the trigger. The Mech was hit by hundreds of rounds. They smashed into its torso and cut deep until it was knocked down by the sheer weight of ammunition. Antos rushed to it and placed his barrel against the flowing heart plate and fired three times until it went limp, but Taylor went right for Rocha. He turned her over to see was gone. He put a finger to her pulse, and there was nothing. He wanted to tell himself that she wasn't dead.

Now he felt sick to his stomach.

"Taylor, we have to move!" Jones shouted.

But Taylor didn't even hear him. He put his gloved hand onto her cheek and stroked it.

"Why couldn't I save you?"

Jones reached Taylor and shook him by his shoulder.

"Colonel, we have to go now!"

He slowly shook his head.

"Let the drones take her."

But Taylor ignored him, picked her up, and threw her body over his shoulder. He turned and watched Jones pick up the hammer from the fallen Mech and continue to lead the way.

They rushed on room after room until they reached the access point where they had come through. The body of the fallen fighter had already been ferried inside the Sky King. Gunfire rang out at their backs and Jones turned to face it as Taylor carried on with Rocha's body. Babacan stopped at the entrance to the room with Jones and opened fire with the Hydra in one last salvo to buy them some time. The two of them rushed to the door and climbed aboard.

Hariz was looking back to Taylor for an order, but she got nothing and could only just make out the body of Rocha resting in Taylor's arms.

"Go!" Jones screamed.

It was all the prompting she needed. She released the clamps from the enemy ship and put the power down so that they raced off from the surface, banking hard to come around on course to the Guam. Jones looked down at Taylor and came close to tears on seeing the toll it had taken on him. He could now see that the Colonel wasn't the heartless machine he presented himself as. In that one look Jones saw it all. Taylor felt everything, but he bottled it up for the benefit of all those he commanded.

Taylor's connection to this new world had finally felt real as the same heart wrenching tragedies struck at his core once again. Hariz looked over her shoulder at Taylor once more and felt her heart sink when she saw him holding the dead woman in his arms. She wanted nothing more than to go to him, but she had to return to her controls. Jones instead sat down beside Taylor and rested his hand on his shoulder.

"There was nothing you could have done."

Taylor shook his head.

"Don't ever tell me that. Our fate is never sealed. Of course there was something I could have done. All she wanted was to follow me and be one of us. Why did I take her away from all that she had?"

"You know that with this war there will be many more personnel and civilians called up to fight. You've seen that before. Rocha would likely have met her end in this war sometime or other."

Jones was shocked that this seemed to hit him so hard after all the death he had encountered and lived through. They felt the undercarriage hit the landing bad back aboard the Guam, but it was a bittersweet return. Jones hit the door switch, and the ramp lowered. Several corpsmen waiting for them, but it was pointless. Taylor got up with Rocha still held in his arms and stepped out with a war weary pace. His face was like stone, and everybody stayed clear until he reached one of the stretchers waiting on the deck. He gently placed her down.

Taylor looked at the body for just a few moments before turning and heading for the bridge. Jones followed close behind but did not say a word. They got onto the bridge to find the fleet still hammering the battleship they had boarded. Doing enough damage to look like a determined attack, but not enough to stop her from jumping out.

"Is it done?" Cohen asked, turning to face Taylor. She froze when she saw his stony face.

"Yes," replied Taylor firmly.

"Losses?"

"Two dead, five wounded."

Cohen could see he didn't want to talk about it so turned back to the battle.

"Their Primary systems just went back online," said Nichols.

"Come on, jump," said Cohen.

The ship began to shimmer and then finally vanished.

"We got it. Prepare to jump. Get us the hell out of here, and inform Eme that we are good to go!"

Cohen turned back to Taylor now.

"I am so sorry for the loss of your people, Colonel. They will not be forgotten."

"That much I can guarantee," he replied.

"There will be many more losses in this war, but none of them will ever be easy," said Cohen. But she quickly realised how petty she sounded as she remembered Taylor's past, "I'm sorry, I know…"

"It's okay. Sometimes there just comes a point where enough is enough. We are going to win this war. I know because failure is not an option, but the price will be more than any of you could ever have imagined."

It was a grim outlook, but nobody doubted him.

"So celebrate this small victory, as they are the few moments of pleasure you will get in life from now on."

"Ready to jump," said Nichols.

"Then take us home…jump."

CHAPTER TEN

The jump home should have been a triumphant one, but the first sight before them was the crippled Cholan fleet that had been the decoy. The Nakbe had made it but was badly damaged, and their fleet was half what it had been.

"My word, they took a beating," said Jones.

"Of course, how else do you think we bought the time we needed?"

Jones turned to Taylor.

"You knew they were going to take a beating?"

"And anyone who thought otherwise was deluding themselves."

"And you don't think they deserved to know that?"

"It's a simple numbers game. We take small losses now, or we take greater losses later."

"And you can be that cold about it?"

"Cold?" Taylor asked, "There is nothing cold about wanting to save as many as I can."

Jones stopped to think it over but decided to let it go. "So how sure are you that this worked?"

"You can keep asking me, but I don't know any more than you. They won't put anything out across open channels. Only a handful of people in this fleet knew our real mission. We won't know till we talk to Irala in person."

"So what now?"

"Find out if it really did work, and see if the President's promise of all the resources he could give is actually true. Let's go."

They got back to the fighter bays and found Rocha's body still lay where Taylor had left it. He walked past and looked at her, but continued right on to the transport. Hariz was waiting at the entrance for him, and he could see the look of sadness on her face. But she was not sad for the losses of the two marines, but for how her heart ached for him.

"Hariz, we need a ride, right now," he said, as he and Jones stepped up to pass her on the ramp. She reached out and brushed her hand across his arm.

"Alita," she replied. He turned, and his eyes met with hers for just a split second.

"Get us in the air, Lieutenant!" he ordered as he got inside.

Taylor and Jones sat down opposite each other, and she stepped past to reach the controls.

"The Lieutenant there has taken quite a liking to you."

Taylor shrugged.

"What? You don't like her?"

"You don't fraternise with colleagues."

"Maybe not in your day, but it is openly encouraged now. And anyway, I know plenty of your history. You were with an NCO in your very own Regiment, weren't you? Got you into a little trouble, from what I remember," he replied with a smile.

But Taylor was not amused, and Jones understood how insensitive he was being as he realised how much Taylor had lost.

They came aboard the Ares colony quickly and were escorted directly to the conference room where Taylor had devised the plan to begin with. They entered to find the discussions had broken down, and many of the representatives were shouting at each other so loudly it was hard to distinguish one argument from another.

"What the hell are they doing?"

"Turning on each other," replied Taylor.

They watched and waited for a few moments, hoping for it to return to calm, but they had no such luck. The President was slumped in his seat silently as one of his aides argued with the Cholan Ambassador. Then Jafar stood up and entered the debate. His voice carried louder and farther than any other.

"Enough!"

The room fell silent as Jafar pointed for Taylor to come forward.

"Please, Colonel Taylor, tell us the outcome of your mission."

"It was successful," he replied abruptly, "And Irala's part?"

"We are still waiting and praying for news from the Councillor," said Isaacs softly.

"Praying?" Taylor spat out, "We send people out there to their deaths, and you're praying? Quit that bullshit!"

Isaacs suddenly woke up and seemed to take Taylor's comments to heart, as did several others. Taylor looked to Jafar, but he only shrugged.

"What else are we to do but pray for their souls?" Isaacs insisted.

"What else? Help them in life, and save others."

"Only God can do that. He is our only saviour now."

Taylor looked at Jones in despair, as it was the first he had heard of such religious devotion in a long while. He could see Jones didn't agree, but neither was he surprised.

"Has life really gone to shit that much since I've been away?"

"Do you believe in nothing?"

Taylor didn't much like the President's tone, and he could not help but rise to the debate.

"Nothing? I believe in my friends, and what I can do with my own hands. Where is your god now? Where is he in your greatest time of need? Because he sure never showed up in the last few thousand years to help anyone."

"We cannot ever fully understand his plan."

"Right now I'd say if he had a plan, it's to wipe out all civilised life in the universe."

"If that is his will, then we must obey it."

"Fuck that," replied Taylor rather abruptly.

He could feel his blood boil now. He wanted nothing more than to run across the room and smack some sense into the man, but he restrained himself and continued on only with words.

"Maybe it is the plan, but I can't be a part of it. I shouldn't even be in this time and place. But I sure intend to make a difference."

"We should never have woken you up. All you have done is meddle in this Alliance, just as you did in your own time!" Isaacs shouted.

Taylor could see the President was getting desperate

now and just using him as the target of his angst. He opened his mouth to speak again but felt Jones' hand on his shoulder. The Lieutenant leaned in and whispered in his ear.

"We don't need this kind of trouble in our lives. It can lead nowhere good."

Taylor smiled; it sounded just like the sort of sense Charlie would have talked, and he nodded in agreement. As he looked back up, Irala's hologram appeared, and everyone's attention turned to the Aranui Councillor.

"Councillor, do you have news?" Isaacs asked.

"We have successfully tracked the navigation hub, or portal."

Nobody spoke for a moment. Taylor couldn't tell if those around him were welcoming the news or not.

"Is this not what you wanted to hear?" Irala asked, somewhat confused by their response.

"They've lost their balls," replied Taylor, "A few losses and they're rattled."

"A few losses?" Isaacs asked in amazement.

"Don't patronise me. I was actually there. My people spilt blood for this, and I lost a friend to achieve what we needed to do. So don't even dare lecture me on loss."

"Colonel, I must ask you to change your tone."

"Yeah, good luck with that," Jones whispered to himself as Taylor went on.

"You told me I would have every resource I needed to make this work. Was that promise a lie?"

Isaacs sat back down and sighed, for he was already regretting having given such an assurance.

"Don't tell me we sacrificed all that for nothing!"

"Lord Jafar, what do you think?" Isaacs asked.

"That our planned course of action was the only way. We must stay the course."

Taylor could almost hear himself in his old friend.

"Then you would have us throw everything into this operation? An operation that could leave us defenceless if it fails?"

"If there was a perfect path, we would have tread it already," added Irala.

"Let us do this," Taylor said, almost begging, "Give me what I need, and I will make this happen."

Isaacs looked sick to his stomach.

"I will join you," said Jafar, "I will command the Krys element of the fleet that takes on this task."

"Lord Jafar, you are required here. You must send some other in your stead."

But he ignored the comment.

"Who else will join me?"

"My people know that this must be done. We will give all that we can," Irala answered him.

Admiral Eme finally spoke up. "If this is the only way I can help my people, then you will have the Nakbe and the remainder of the fleet under my command."

Taylor looked to the President now and pleaded with him.

"Please, give us the support we need, and let us stem the tide before it is too late."

He nodded in agreement and appeared relieved to finally pass over the burden to others.

"You will have it."

"How long will it take to finish repairs on the Nakbe and assemble the rest of the fleet?" Taylor asked.

"Forty-eight hours," Jafar answered.

"Then that's when we go."

* * *

The Immortals were formed up before the coffins of their two fallen comrades awaiting their cremation and for Taylor to speak some words. He stood between the coffins. He paced along their length and ran his hands down both of them. He turned to address his comrades.

"Rocha and Preito. They fought and fell honourably. Death will come to us all, so never fear it. Embrace it. The fighter who fears death will bring it upon themselves sooner than they deserve. Let yourselves dream of what life could be like without this, but never forget, this are your life now. Take everything you can from it - every shred of good, every laugh and joke, every drink with friends, and every triumphant kill. This is what you live for. Rocha and Preito are gone from this life, but they will remain Immortals forever."

He took his position beside the others and Jones could see the pain and anguish was all but gone from his eyes. They watched the bodies move through a tunnel entrance, and the door closed down in front of them. They held their heads low and waited. Taylor then turned and left. He didn't even give the order for them to do so.

"Detail fallout," Jones said quickly and hurried on after the Colonel.

"Where are you going?"

Taylor shrugged. "Nowhere very much. What is there to do now but wait?"

"That kind of tension could break a man."

Taylor nodded. "It can and it does."

"Then follow me."

Taylor looked at him in surprise but was curious enough to do so. Jones led him to Zenobia's Garden. Taylor was initially weary and thought Jones was playing a joke on him.

"What is this?" he asked suspiciously.

"For all the time you have spent in space, I know your heart remains on Earth. So go inside, and remember what it is you have fought for."

"But that isn't real."

"It's as real as your mind wants it to be."

He thought about turning and leaving, but somehow found himself stepping inside. The smells and sights he had always loved so much instantly hit him. It felt real in every way as his feet passed over soft grass and dirt, and he took in a deep breath of cool air, feeling the wind on his skin.

"Impressive isn't it?"

"Very."

They walked on for twenty metres, and Taylor was amazed to feel so many of his worries and thoughts just vanish. They came to a bench that looked like it was cut from stone, but he knew it couldn't be. He took a seat, and Jones sat down beside him. It was both bizarre and fascinating all at once.

"Reminds me of France."

"Where you fought?"

"That's not what I meant. Where Charlie Jones once lived between the wars."

Jones was surprised. "What was he doing there? I was told he never left the Regiment from the day he signed up."

Taylor shook his head.

"He'd just seen and been through too much. After his capture, he was a wreck, and he never fully recovered from that. No one truly knows what really happened to him, what tortures he endured."

"I didn't know any of this."

"Yeah, well the grim details can often get lost in a sexed up history. Charlie left the life and settled down to become nothing more than a humble farmer, and he loved it."

"What changed?"

"I needed him, and eventually, he came back to us."

"So you blame yourself for his loss as well?"

"No, to suggest he shouldn't have been in that war would do a disservice to all that he achieved."

"You know I read so much about Charlie Jones and the Immortals, but I am starting to get the sense that there is so much more to know."

"It doesn't matter anymore. It's long gone."

"It does matter. It's why you are here today. Your last action in that life was to fight Lord Erdogan himself. You defeated him in personal combat. You won, how did you do it?"

Taylor shook his head. "I could never win that battle. He was too strong, too fast. Even with a dozen of the best fighters I have ever known at my side, we were being cut to pieces."

He was picturing it now. As for him, it was just a few days before. He remembered every detail in vivid and graphic detail.

"So tell me about it."

"I gave in. Let him strike when he thought I would move, to reel him in. I had to accept my own death to defeat him. It was the only way."

"And yet here you are, healthier than ever."

"By some freakish development of science. You know sometimes it is best to not meddle. Clones were a case in point."

"Yes, they have never been legal in the Alliance. Lord Jafar had all cloning facilities destroyed soon after your war ended."

"This Bolormaa that Councillor Irala tells us of. Do you really believe she is so single-mindedly sadistic as he suggests?"

"I've got no idea, but I'm sure we'll find out soon enough."

"Come on, join us for a drink. We will drink to our fallen friends," said Jones.

They carried on to the bar they had been the night before and stopped as they looked on at how heaving it was with serving personnel.

"I think you've started something here, Colonel." Jones said.

They went inside and took a seat amongst the rest of their unit. Once again Alita came to his side, and he attempted to brush her off.

"I never thought I would see the day when I could say I served with Colonel Mitch Taylor of the Immortals," she said, smiling as she rested her arm on top of his.

He moved his hand away, but Jones noticed.

"What did you tell us only today?" Jones asked, "To take every moment of joy we can get in this life. Don't fall back on your advice just yet."

Taylor thought about it for a moment and slowly turned to look at her. She was undressing him with her starry eyes.

"What are you waiting for, Colonel?" Antos asked, with a big grin on his face, "When a smoking hot pilot offers to take you for a ride, there's only one answer."

Taylor knocked back a drink in one and laughed. He put his arm around her as they stood up together.

"You get hold of me if there is any news whatsoever, you hear?" he said to Jones.

"You got it, boss."

He looked at Alita, who was staring back at him, and leaned in to kiss her. It was met with a round of applause started by Jones.

Taylor smiled and dropped his arm to her lower back to lead her out.

* * *

Taylor awoke in a sweat as he imagined Erdogan's blade driving through his chest. His eyelids snapped open, and he was breathing heavily. It startled the woman lying next to him, and for a moment he thought to call her Eli, but when he looked over to her, he remember it wasn't.

"Are you okay?" she asked.

She lay naked beside him on top of his left arm. She was beautiful and appeared entirely besotted with him. Her eyes seemed to pierce to his brain, and her face turned quickly to concern as if she was seeing right into his thoughts.

"What can I do?"

But he shook his head. He slipped his arm out from under her and got off the tiny bed that they had just squeezed into.

"What's wrong? What did I do?"

He grabbed his uniform and began to pull it on as she sat up and waited for his response.

"Nothing at all. I am sorry. I just need some space."

"Do you regret doing this?"

"No, not as long as you don't. But there are some wounds that never heal."

"Parker?" she asked.

Taylor shook his head. "Jones has a damn big mouth."

"I've wanted this from the moment I saw you. I wasn't scared when we were on the way to that battleship because I knew you were with me."

"And this society has no issue with this at all. You know how much shit I got in for fooling around with one of my marines?"

She shook her head.

"I go away for a few hundred years, and you've turned into a load of hippies."

She looked confused.

"Don't worry, it's before even my time."

She only smiled back anyway.

"You know what is so painful when you start to get attached to those you go to war with?"

"No," she whispered.

"That you have to accept that you will lose any and all of those you care for."

"And you care for me?"

"I care for all of you. We are a family now. I will do everything in my power to protect you, but that isn't enough."

"You told us to enjoy the time we have, and I intend to do just that."

Taylor pulled on his boots and nodded in agreement

before leaving his room with her still inside. He knew she was completely blinded by the lust she felt for him. It was a relief to once again be close to someone, but it wasn't what he really needed. That was gone for good.

A day without action made him feel restless. His mind was wandering to a depth of misery and depression that could break him apart if he dwelled on it for any length of time. He increased his pace and just kept walking until he reached the gymnasium and realised exactly what he needed. He stepped inside and found it completely abandoned, as he was hoping it would be.

As he walked towards a heavy bag, he pulled off his shirt and let it drop at his feet. He wanted nothing more than to get some aggression out now. As he closed the distance, he swung a heavy hook as hard as he could and it smashed into the bag. He followed it with another and another, until he was hitting one after the other with barely a moment to breathe. After a few minutes when he was warm and sweating, he stopped for a moment and paced around. He came to a standstill; noticing Jafar was standing at the door.

"I never believed I would once again be able to go into battle with you."

"Yeah, well I never expected to live to see a day like this," replied Taylor.

"I'm glad you are. We need champions like you at times like these," he replied and slowly paced towards the Colonel while he landed a few more punches on the bag at a more relaxed pace.

"I have it all, old friend. Everything. All I wanted to do was die and know that everything was going to be okay. But it isn't okay. Everything is not okay. It's fucked beyond belief. And now I am stuck out of my own time. Do you know how cruel it was to bring me back now, how selfish it was? Should have switched the machine off and let me go with dignity."

"You don't believe that."

"No?" Taylor snapped.

"You fought like a legend to survive, and now you have."

"Yeah, well this isn't what I signed up for," he replied and continued hammering into the bag.

"And when you were born, did you choose that time and place also?"

Taylor stopped. It was bizarre to hear Jafar speak more like Irala might, but his alien friend went on before he could say anything.

"You did not choose your first life. But you did what you always told us to do. Improvise and overcome. Now you have been resurrected into different life that is not of your choosing either. Only this time you have another lifetime of experience and knowledge. Whatever created you in this universe, you were made to be a fighter and a survivor."

Taylor hit the bag a few more times, knowing he was being thrown the sort of logic he would have always used back at him. His punches began to slow in speed and power until finally he stopped altogether. Jafar was smiling at him, and that lifted his spirits.

"So I'm back and you can't resist getting in on the action?"

"There hasn't been this much excitement in my life since the day Erdogan died. I feel alive once more. So it's time for you to be the warrior I know you used to be."

Taylor stepped over to Jafar and tapped him on the shoulder in a friendly gesture.

"Okay, okay. You got me."

CHAPTER ELEVEN

Seven hours until departure.

Taylor sat in the co-pilot's seat of Alita's Sky King as they soared through the fleet towards the Guam. The fleet had been gaining in size every hour and now stood at over one hundred warships and their support craft.

"They could assemble all this, why didn't they last time around?" Taylor asked.

He meant it rhetorically, but Alita jumped in with a response anyway.

"They were scared of throwing everything in. Aren't you?"

He shook his head.

"When you know it's the only way, all fear goes out the window."

"So we make this work or it's the end of us all? It can't be that bad."

"From what Irala tells us, it is that bad. This enemy is far beyond what we are capable of dealing with right now, maybe ever. We've encountered just minor elements of their true strength and every time came off worse."

"How do you manage it?" she asked.

"What?"

"To shoulder the burden of everything? Of all the worlds and races. You have lived in this time for so few days, and yet you have risen to lead it."

"I'm not leading this," he replied modestly.

"But you are the driving force behind it all."

"I never wanted to be."

But he could see she was too enthralled by his power and authority to stop smiling.

"When we get into this fight, you only do your job, nothing more. No stupid heroics," he added, starting to feel responsible for her.

That made her blush, but it wasn't his intention.

"Is that what you do? Never put yourself out for others? You have never done anything stupid for the people you care for?"

"His career was built on such experiences," said Jones, leaning in between the two of them.

Taylor could not disagree.

"But I don't ask anyone to do more than their job. Fight for each other, protect each other, but don't ever throw your lives away."

They passed through into the landing bays of the Guam and came to a perfectly smooth and soft landing this time.

"You know you could have ridden this out on any ship in the fleet. Why stay on this one?"

"Told you before, she's carried us through enough shit already. She has kept us safe and kept us moving. There is a lot to be said for that."

"Not getting sentimental, are you?"

Taylor laughed. "Nothing wrong with sentiment, Jones. Just too much that you can't afford to lose can drag you down to a state of misery I would wish on nobody. But while the Guam still flies and her Commander will still have us, this is our home."

They stepped off the craft to see a Krys vessel being unloaded beside them. Two Mech warriors were carrying what Taylor knew to be the weapon Jafar had promised him. It looked like a steel dome almost as tall as a Human being. It was carried in a strong cradle with a Mech at each end.

"So that's it, a planet killing weapon?" Jones asked.

"Sadly this ain't the first time I have seen one, but it will be the first time I have used one."

Irala's hologram appeared next to the weapon and took a few paces closer to Taylor.

"So this gonna do it, Irala?"

"Yes. By our estimations, this weapon will do far more than just destroy the navigation portal. It will make the world uninhabitable for a long time to come. The technology of jump navigation is highly advanced and difficult to achieve. If you succeed, it will ensure the Morohta will be unable to reach us for some time."

"You're sure about that?"

Irala nodded.

"I sure hope you're right because we could just be jumping into the lion's mouth."

"I wish you every luck with it, and will do everything in my power to make sure you succeed."

"You will be there?"

"I must. There is nothing more important in our lives than this."

That meant a lot to Taylor; he knew how weary the Aranui were of risking the few people they had left. Before he could say another word, Irala vanished.

"You nervous yet?" Taylor asked Jones as they watched the Krys warriors place the weapon down.

"Flying into unknown space with the most powerful weapon I have ever seen, against a terrifying enemy, and know that if we fail we all die? Nervous doesn't even begin to describe it."

"We'll have plenty of help. We're dropping onto the surface in our thousands. We're just the ones delivering this bad boy."

He turned around to find the rest of their team there and waiting for his orders.

"Get this weapon loaded on the boat."

"No," replied Alita.

Taylor was stunned at her response but then saw her pointing across the hangar bay. He followed the line of her arm until he was looking at a craft twice its size. It had an almost fist-like prow that looked very thickly armoured. A single massive engine almost as wide as the fuselage protruded from the rear. Four small wings housed smaller V-tol thrusters. Every part of the craft looked designed to take a beating. Even the wings were heavily reinforced to the hull. On the chin of the vessel was a weapon that was an even larger version of the Hydra cannon.

It was an angry-looking craft that looked like it wanted to smash all that was before it, and that made Taylor smile. It reminded him of the Mastiffs that they had used successfully on so many missions before.

"What the hell is that?"

"The finest and toughest transport you've ever seen,"

replied Alita, "She is a Bullnose Stomer, but I like to call her Brunhild. She will see us through anything."

"Okay then, get her loaded and ready to go. When all this finally gets started, it's gonna happen quicker than any of you can imagine."

He turned and headed for the bridge with Jones.

"Welcome aboard, Colonel," Cohen said as he entered.

The Commander's tone was the polar opposite of the cold shoulder he had been given when he first arrived.

"Are you ready for this?" Taylor asked.

"Everything is set to go. All we are waiting on is the last remaining ships."

Taylor was anxious now as he looked down at the time on his console.

"What is it?"

"Just don't like sitting around waiting when there is a job to be done."

"Our time will come soon enough, can we not enjoy this moment of peace?"

Taylor shook his head. "When we're back and have completed out mission, then is the time."

An alarm sounded out, and both of them turned to Nichols for answers.

"I'm getting energy signature readings all over the place."

"No," replied Cohen, shaking.

There were glimmers of movement on the view screen, and suddenly eight Morohta battleships appeared before them with dozens of escort frigates twenty klicks from their position.

"How can this be?" Cohen asked, feeling her pulse race, "Shields up! All crew to their stations. Prepare to repel borders!"

Nichols began to implement the commands, but Taylor interrupted.

"Get me Jafar, now!" he said sternly.

Nichols looked to Cohen for confirmation, and she quickly nodded.

The alien Lord was immediately projected before him.

"We cannot afford this, Jafar."

"Then what?"

Taylor tried desperately to think of an answer.

"The Cholan fleet is retreating!"

"What the hell are they doing?" Cohen asked, her voice now desperate.

"Get me Admiral Eme!" Taylor said firmly.

Eme was quickly displayed, and Jafar remained standing and watching everything unfold.

"What are you doing, Admiral? This is no time to cut and run!" Taylor demanded.

"I am sorry, Colonel, but you cannot win this. You are living in a dream world where you would see us all destroyed."

"You what? No...you gave the Morohta our location?"

"If my people are to survive, we must side with the strongest race here, and that is not Human, Aranui, or Krycenaean. We must survive. Good luck, Colonel, and I hope you do the best thing for your people, as I have been compelled to do."

He couldn't believe what he was hearing.

"Taylor, we cannot win this fight," said Jafar.

He already knew it, and they watched the Nakbe moved out of formation with the few support vessels she had left.

"Fools," said Taylor.

"We are being hailed by one of the Morohta vessels," said Jafar.

"Don't answer, not yet," replied Taylor.

"So what do you want to do?"

"Are we ready to jump?"

Jafar looked at him, confused.

"Yes, but with little over half the fleet we expected, and how can we leave this enemy fleet here?"

"We're not going to. Prepare to jump, and wait for my command. The world where this navigation portal is, what is its name?"

Jafar was surprised, but he did not hesitate to take the order from Taylor and promptly answered, "The world is called Khar Els."

"And that is what they will know and recognise it as?"

"They will know, yes."

"Then put me through with these assholes."

They did as he said, and a screen projected before them. It was just as Jones had seen before, a deep dark blackness with just two faint eyes staring at them. Taylor stepped forward confidently to the display to attract attention to himself.

"Hey, you ugly son of a bitch. Bolormaa is it, or one of her minions? I've got some news for you."

The eyes suddenly drew slightly closer to the screen and focused onto Taylor.

"That's right. You fucked with the wrong people. You haven't come here to destroy us; we are going to destroy you. I hear the world of Khar Els is more than a little important to you. Well I'm gonna give it a visit, and I'm going to be sure to leave a path of destruction in my wake.

I'll see you there."

The alien eyes expanded in surprise, and Taylor smiled, knowing he had got their attention. He turned back to Jafar.

"Jump!"

A gateway flashed open ahead of them, and they soared forward into it while the enemy vessels were trying to get their first shots off. One of the battleships fired on a frigate that was between them and the Guam. The impact ripped a hole in the hull, and two shots from two other vessels caused it to explode in a flash of light. The Guam reached the gateway, and they knew they were safe, but not for long.

"You sure know how to make friends," joked Jones.

"You want us to be both the bait and the mission, you know how unlikely that is to work?"

"Got a better idea, Commander, let me know. I'm doing what I can with what we've got."

"Think they'll take the bait?"

"Damn right they will, Jones. I just bruised their ego. They will not stand to let us strike at their heart."

"So the best thing you could think of was to bring everything down on our heads?"

"It was the only thing."

They passed through the gateway and came out in full view of Khar Els. It was a vibrant blue planet with what looked like at least eighty percent water coverage. Even the land glowed a beautiful blue azure. It was breathtaking to behold.

"My word," said Cohen, "And we have to destroy it?"

"Them or us," replied Taylor, "Get us to the surface, and give us as much time as you can."

"It's gonna be a rough ride."

They were closing on the planet quickly now. They could see a small defence grid of two rings running around it. As they neared, the Aranui vessels opened fire with their beam weapons, smashing the structure with a volley of devastating fire until it began to break apart and collapse into orbit.

"I'm getting energy readings. We've got incoming!" Nichols called out.

"Good, then we've pulled them away from our Solar System," replied Taylor.

They watched the display screens as the fleet they had encountered just moments before materialised in an attempt to block their path to the surface, but the Allied fleet of the three races continued to surge forward at full speed. Almost one hundred vessels approached as one.

"Weapons free, launch fighters, open fire!" Cohen ordered.

The fleet opened fire almost in perfect sequence, but the enemy ships were gaining power to fire their vast ordnance.

"What if we get hit by that?" Jones asked Taylor.

"Better hope that we don't. They have no idea of our plan, or of the weapon we are carrying."

"So we just hope to survive this?"

Taylor nodded.

Bursts of energy soared from the vast Morohta battleships, and two ships in the fleet were blown apart instantly. The Guam took a hit from one of the enemy frigates but managed to brush it off. They were closing on the enemy fleet at a rapid pace now, as they'd been forced to jump into such a narrow space. The battleships could not regain charge in time, and they watched the screens as the Allied fleet zoomed through the Morohta vessels. Cohen brought up a rear display screen, and they could see the battleships banking to come around, and many of their own fleet was turning to face them.

"How long until we can drop?"

"We must ensure you are safe from ground fire before setting you loose, Colonel," replied Cohen.

As they closed on the planet, they could see a single massive complex on one of the few landmasses on the surface. It was a round structure several kilometres wide and looked like a fortress. There appeared to be twenty towers around the perimeter and dome roof, with a central column rising into the sky that was a hundred metres wide.

"That must be a landing zone," said Jones, pointing to the central structure.

"Sure you want to be putting down? Looks exposed."

"We don't have a lot of choice, but I'd sure appreciate you softening them up first."

"Will do, Colonel. Get to your transport. I'll give you the go when we're ready."

Taylor gestured for Jones to follow him. They got to a quick jogging pace and headed to the landing bays. They felt the Guam rock as she was struck by enemy fire, but nothing so heavy as to slow her down.

"You ever done something as crazy as this before?" Jones asked.

"Yeah," he replied quickly.

"So you're confident about this, right? I mean you've done it all before?"

"Confident? Not really. But I'll do everything in my power to make it work."

"I don't want to die here today."

"None of us do, Jones."

They reached the landing bay. The side door of Brunhild was open and their team loaded and ready to go. Another two of the same craft sat nearby to fly in support of them. They ran inside and jumped into their seats. Alita was at the single pilot's seat that was placed between the lines of passenger seats. There was no physical screen or view out of the ship; only video feeds in every direction.

"She really as tough as you say?" Taylor asked.

"Damn right she is. Designed to operate in the worst of environments, she'll take almost anything."

"Yeah, well let's not put that to the test too much."

"You got it, boss."

He sat back now and watched the seconds pass by on his console.

"How did you know they'd take the bait?"

Taylor laughed at Jones. "You never know many things that are for certain in this life. I took a calculated guess. Piss someone off enough, and they tend to want to take a swing at you."

"You know you've probably just painted a target on your own back?"

"Probably, but that would be nothing new."

Cohen's voice came in over the comms, "You are good to go, Colonel! Good luck!"

Taylor simply nodded to Alita and she knew what to do. She hit the door close switch, and the ramp slammed shut as they lifted off the deck and soared out into space. They were met by the warming sight of dozens more craft like their own, as well as almost fifty Sky Kings, and with many more at their backs. Hundreds of Human and Krys warriors were on their way to the surface, and all around them the gun batteries of the fleet above were laying down a carpet of fire on the enemy structure below.

As Brunhild began breaking through the world atmosphere, they could see that two of the towers of the structure had been badly damaged, but the canopies of the rest slid open, and bursts of light rushed towards them.

"Incoming!" Alita shouted.

One of the pulses burst over the nose of their craft and shook them violently, but it seemed to do no damage at all. Alita targeted the nearest tower and reached for the trigger on the joystick before her. She squeezed it, and the screen in front of her lit up as tracer fire surged towards the target.

"Woohoo!" she yelled excitedly as she blew the gun system apart.

She moved onto the next target as Taylor watched the bombardment continue. Several Sky Kings blew up around them, but their frontal armour appeared all but impervious to the enemy's weapons.

"This ain't so bad!"

Even as the words rolled off her tongue, she noticed a larger weapon system open up on the side of the main tower. It was a huge single barrelled cannon that appeared to be tracking and targeting them personally.

"Hang on!" she shouted and banked quickly. The gun fired and narrowly missed them, but they had to turn sharply on approach as the shots followed their path.

"We're okay. We're okay!"

Then they felt a massive hit strike their flank and rip a hole in the fuselage. One of the team was sucked out, along with the bomb. It flew out before anyone could react.

"No!" Taylor screamed.

He rushed to the breach and almost instinctively leapt out, but then he remembered their new suits did not have any drop or jump capability.

"Fuck! Fuck!"

He looked around through the breach for some sign of the device, but it was gone, despite the fact they were only a few hundred metres above the ground now.

"Take us down!"

But before Alita could respond, they were hit by three more shots that rocked them, and Taylor fell towards the hole in the hull. Just as he was about to fall, he felt someone grasp his leg and haul him back inside. It was Babacan. The alien was holding on to him tight as they thundered towards the enemy structure. Taylor could just make out on Alita's screen that she was heading right for the roof of the central tower, yet they had no way to slow down. Babacan pushed Taylor into the seat beside him and hit the restraints on. Secure metal bands locked around all of the occupants just in time.

"This is gonna hurt!" she yelled.

They smashed into the roof and crashed through the surface before grinding to a quick halt.

"Everyone out!" Taylor ordered.

He released the bands and jumped out of the breach. They had pierced just the first level of the structure, and the engines of Brunhild still protruded from the roof.

"Come on, let's go, go, go!"

As they clambered out, they heard gunfire erupt from sentry guns further into the room. Taylor hit his shield on barely in time as two of the shots hit it, and Babacan's

Hydra quickly replied to the sound. The dim room lit up as he destroyed both weapons in a single burst.

"That was a pretty pathetic attempt at security," said Jones.

"I guess when you're the ultimate badass in the universe, you probably don't feel you have to worry much about people coming and fucking with you. We're probably the only aliens to ever step foot here," replied Taylor.

He looked back to Brunhild. Alita was waiting in the doorway with her carbine in hand. "You're coming with us. We'll just have to find another way out."

"Do you think that's likely to happen?"

"Damn right, Jones. I don't intend on dying on this world."

He lifted up his comms unit, "Jafar, this is Taylor, come in."

"What is it, Taylor?"

"The device, can it survive a fall of a few hundred metres?"

"What?" Jafar responded loudly.

"Well, can it?"

"Yes, the cradle allows it to be dropped from orbit as is, but it is single use. One descent, it will be fine. But have you lost..."

"We're okay. Don't worry about it," Taylor interrupted him and ended the transmission.

"Track it, now!" he shouted to Jones.

"On it!"

* * *

"Has Taylor just lost the device?"

"I've no idea, Sarik, but we must trust in him."

A claxon resonated throughout the ship, and Jafar turned to see two hull breaches on the screen.

"We've been boarded!" Sarik shouted.

Before Jafar could respond, they heard gunfire not far from their position. He stepped over to his chair and lifted out the huge glaive standing beside it. He turned back to the entrance to the bridge just in time to see one of the Stalkers run at him. He swung the glaive around so that the solid steel counterweight smashed into the Stalker's head. The impact was so strong it was thrown sideways across the room, and its legs collapsed under it. Jafar kept swinging the weapon and finally brought the blade end down onto the torso of the creature. The edge lit up like an Assegai tip and pierced the body right through, the blade hitting the deck below.

"Sweep the ship now, Sarik!"

* * *

"I've got it," said Jones.

He showed Taylor the console on his arm. It looked like it had dropped inside the complex between the outer walls and central tower.

"Not too far away, let's go," replied Taylor.

They rushed out of the room and found a ramp that circled around the inner tower. It had no floors and was hollow inside.

"Whoa!" Jones shouted as he came to a standstill. The spiralled ramp looked organic and had no barrier of any kind. It was just two metres wide and seemingly led all the way to the base, "What the hell is this?"

Taylor looked to the very base and could see what appeared to be a vast barrel looking up at them.

"If I had to guess, I'd say it's a weapon."

"What? A weapon for what?"

Taylor shrugged, went forward, and led the way down. He was still surprised to see so little resistance, but glad of it, too. As they got half way down, he stopped on seeing an opening that led outside. He cautiously stepped out and looked around. A maze of metallic causeways ran out to each of the towers. Each causeway was five metres wide, but he stopped when he saw what was up ahead. He spotted the weapon they had lost. It was balanced precariously on the edge of one of the causeways.

"All right, got it," replied Taylor as they went forward. They rushed out along the causeway in what was a completely exposed environment, but they knew they had no choice. Enemy fighters flew past overhead with friendlies hot on their tails. As they drew nearer, the causeway began to creep, and the device appeared to tilt and slip a little. Taylor came to an abrupt standstill and raised his hand for others to do the same. They watched in horror as it swayed from one side to another. Taylor looked down. It was several hundred metres to the next level, and the cradle of the device looked badly damaged from the impact it had taken.

"We can't risk it falling. We don't know if it will survive."

He took off his rifle and laid it down before beginning a slow creep towards the device. He could hear the side railings creek as they began to buckle further. Gunfire and aircraft soared past either side of him, but he slowed his breathing and crept closer and closer. He could feel the causeway beneath him was flexing and moving with the wind, and that only served to panic his nerves further. As he took the last step he needed to, the pressure caused the bomb to slip away from him, and it began to go over the edge. He jumped forward and took hold of one of the grab handles on the cradle, wedging his body against a part of the railing still intact.

As the device tipped, he could feel the strain pulling on him, and he held on with everything he could. It began to drag him over when finally he managed to wedge one foot in a gap between the railing and causeway floor, and the device lurched to a halt. He winced with pain as it began to stretch beyond the limitations of his suit. Jones and Babacan sprinted towards him and pulled the device back onto the causeway. He felt the stress relieved from his body and sighed, lying flat in disbelief.

Jones offered him his hand. He was about to accept when he saw a look of terror on Jones' face. He was looking up and further along the causeway.

"Taylor, we got a problem."

* * *

Jafar picked up a three-barrelled pulse cannon from the stand beside his chair and strode out into the corridor beyond to join the fight. As he entered, he came up against two Morohta soldiers. He aimed at the first and pulled the trigger just once. All three barrels fired like a shotgun and blew the warrior apart. He quickly turned the weapon on the other but found Sarik on the floor nursing a leg wound. Several bodies were around him.

"Ship is over run," he stated.

Jafar didn't want to accept it, but he knew it was the

case. He pulled Sarik up, handed him the weapon, and rushed back to his console. He picked up his glaive once again and punched in a code into the side of his chair. A silver control panel rose out from the armrest. He placed his hand on it and looked back at the screens behind him one last time. The battle was still to be waged. They were buying time for Taylor, but at a wicked price.

"All crew, abandon ship!" he ordered.

He then pressed down on the button, and a counter for a self-destruct sequence began.

"Let's go!"

There were just three crew left on the bridge with him, and they rushed out to help Sarik and waited for him to lead the way. It was a short run to the pods, but they could hear gunfire echo through every corridor. He took a bend and found himself in front of a Stalker. It thrust forward and embedded one of its talons into his chest. He let out a cry of pain and cut down at the leg that had impaled him, cutting it clean from the creature before thrusting deep into its body.

The talon had entered between the chest and shoulder armour and had met little resistance. Blue blood poured down his armour, but he wasn't going to let it stop him. They rushed on to the first escape pod and clambered inside. Gunfire hit the walls as Jafar waited for them all to get in, stepping inside last as two shots hit the frame where he had just been standing. He punched the go button, and they felt the g-force as they blasted off from the stricken vessel.

Jafar turned his attention back to Sarik now, and he appeared to be in as much pain as he was.

"We aren't as fast as we used to be, are we?" Sarik joked.

"Speed isn't everything," Jafar said sternly and began putting out a distress signal on the console on the wall.

"Will they come for us?"

"Yes, Sarik, this war isn't over for us yet," Jafar replied confidently and sat down beside his old friend.

"And you still believe Taylor has got it in him?"

"Taylor is the same man he was the day I met him. He will come through for us."

"How do you know?"

"Because he always has. And if I will choose to have faith in anything in this life, it is in Mitch Taylor."

* * *

Taylor took Jones' hand and was hauled to his feet. He immediately spun around to confront the new threat that seemed to shock Jones so much. He froze, trying to comprehend what he was looking at. A creature blocked their path just ten metres ahead. None of them knew how it managed to get so close, but they had been so busy focusing on the device to notice.

To some degree it resembled a Morohta warrior, but it was almost twice as large. Four legged, but with a humanoid shaped upper torso. Its legs were more like some kind of giant insect, and yet every part of its body was covered in a hard shell that mimicked the colours of its surroundings in a chameleon fashion.

Neither side made an attempt to move as they studied each other. The creature's hands seemed empty and three fingered, but the armoured suit it wore appeared to have the potential to hide a wealth of weapons. Over its head was an oval shell of a helmet that pointed forward at the centre and was pierced elaborately. Taylor knew this was someone important to the Morohta, and the fact it was alone made him doubt if they would be able to defeat it.

"Bolormaa, I assume!"

The helmet on the creature quickly retracted back into its body and revealed a head almost Krys in shape, but a deep dark red skin that was mottled all over.

Ugly motherfucker, Taylor thought.

He recognised the eyes immediately, the same as had plagued them each time they made contact with Morohta ships.

"What do you know of Bolormaa?"

He was surprised to hear a male voice and realised it could not be the infamous alien leader. That was a relief to him. It was a deep imposing voice that reminded him of Erdogan.

"What do I know? Just that she sounds like the bitch of the universe, and I'd like you to give her a message."

He looked down at his console and punched in the codes for a precision aerial strike with two coordinates.

"What message?" the creature asked.

Taylor carried on talking as he used his console and avoided eye contact.

"Just a little message that says fuck you," he replied, accepting the codes on his console.

"You are wasting your time. You will all die."

"My name is Mitch Taylor of Earth, and I am here to tell you that this isn't over. Come for us, and we will take from you more than you ever dreamed possible."

"Small words from a small creature. I could kill you where you stand and all those you bring with you."

"Really? Good to know, but I wasn't wasting my time."

The creature looked confused, but Taylor merely pointed up above him and smiled.

Two missiles from the Guam smashed into the causeway three metres either side of the creature and blew out the section where it stood, causing it to fall through the gap. Taylor rushed to the railings and watched with glee as it fell.

"You're crazy, you know that, right?"

Taylor nodded in approval at Jones and smiled.

"Son of a bitch was boring me to death. Now let's get this done."

CHAPTER TWELVE

The battle was raging all around on the display screens as Jafar lay back against the sidewall of the escape pod. He was shaking his head, wondering how he had gotten to where he was today. His wound still bled, and his comms officer was trying to stop the flow, but he didn't care for it.

"Did we do what Taylor always warned of?" Sarik asked.

"Get soft? Yes. We have gone just the same way his society had before we met humanity. But never think that was a bad thing. We lived good lives for a very long time."

"And you don't enjoy this more than all of the talk and politics we have endured?"

Jafar shrugged. He was not sure anymore. They felt an impact on the edge of the craft and looked up at clamps that had latched on above them.

"Maybe we aren't done yet," said Jafar.

They watched as they were carried and delivered towards the Guam.

"Is this not futile? Even if we survive this, is there any

hope of success against the Morohta?"

"Our people survived a war with them once before, Sarik, and I thought you liked to fight?"

"When there is a chance of winning, yes."

"There is always a chance. Taylor proved that to us. Did we not feel the invincible invaders when we first encountered humanity?"

"Yes, but this is different."

"I do not see how."

It was not long before they docked on the Guam. As they stepped onto the fighter bay decks, there were personnel waiting to offer them assistance. Jafar pointed them to Sarik, but passed them off himself. He strode on through the ship until he reached the bridge.

"Commander, have you anything to report?" he asked Cohen, looking at the battle still unfolding before them.

Cohen looked back and opened her mouth to answer when she saw splashes of blood leading to Jafar and pooling at his feet.

"Please, let us get you medical attention, Lord Jafar."

"Just answer the question."

Cohen looked uncertain.

"I've bled enough in my time to know if I am in trouble. What is Taylor's situation?"

"He has recovered the device but had to call in a strike to deal with something we haven't seen before."

She pressed a few keys and brought up an aerial video feed from the air strike. Jafar shook his head, as he did not recognise it. But a moment later Irala was projected before them.

"It is one of the offspring of Bolormaa," he stated.

"You are sure?" Jafar asked.

"That is what our records indicate. They serve as her leaders and champions, and are not to be toyed with."

"Yeah, well we just dealt with it."

"You killed it?"

Irala watched the replay of the footage and looked unconvinced. In the background they could see dozens of wrecked ships and gunfire and missiles lit up the space all around them. The Guam herself was continuing to take one hit after another from enemy frigates and their fighters.

"How long do we give Taylor?"

"There is no limit, Commander," replied Irala, "For if he fails, we all are finished, anyway."

"So we really are putting our future in twenty men?"

"There are thousands of troops on the surface," Jafar added.

"Yes, but none of them have a device that can end this but Taylor."

"I kept that for a rainy day, as you say. Remember it was the Alliance who decided in their infinite wisdom to outlaw such weapons."

As he finished, a large impact hit the Guam, and they were almost thrown off their feet.

* * *

Taylor crept forward to peer around a corner. He could hear gunfire and took the bend to find a squad of Krys warriors battling the Morohta. He rushed out and crossed behind them to the cover of the next structure. From there he could see an opening inside where the bombardment had created a hole. He rushed inside and was confronted by three Stalkers heading his way to stem the flow.

He fired several shots from the hip, ducking in against a wall to let those behind him get a clear line of sight. They opened fire as he pulled out his Assegai and flicked it open. As the last remaining Stalker came in line with him, he thrust out from the wall and drove it deep. The creature dropped slightly, and he fired three shots into the top of its torso to make sure.

As the body went limp at his feet, he looked at the time once again and realised just how long the fleet had to have been battling the Morohta in orbit above them.

'We have to up this pace!"

He ran on in the direction they had been attacked from.

"How deep do we have to go to get this thing?"

"A long way. Come on, Jones, we have to keep moving!"

They continued on and came to a large tube that appeared to be an elevator.

"Get inside!" Taylor shouted.

Many of them looked suspicious, but they did so anyway. It was twenty metres wide and more likely a vehicle lift than intended for personnel. Taylor looked for the console, but there appeared to be nothing at all. It was Babacan who saw an orifice amongst an organic pipeline running to the ceiling. He put his hand inside without hesitation, and whatever he'd done they began lowering down below the surface at a steady pace that began to increase.

"This part of the plan?"

"Heading below the surface, Jones?"

"No, this elevator."

Taylor looked at him with a smile.

"You know we had no plans on this place, right? We

find a way down. That was the plan."

"Wow, that's it?"

"Hey, that's the way we gotta roll sometimes."

"And were plans always this rudimentary with you?"

"Only when they had to be."

The elevator took them lower and lower as it increased in pace. Taylor was clocking the distance on his console. They were nearly two kilometres below the surface when they began to slow and raised their rifles at the ready for whatever they might have to face.

"No matter what, we go forward, okay?"

Nobody said a word, but he knew they were with him. Finally, the elevator shaft opened up and exposed them to a vast chasm resembling the insides of some titanic creature. The roof and sides were ribbed like a spine and ribs structure, but on the ground there was line after line of light emitting pods twice the size of a man and in a grid formation. There was no movement at all for a second, as if they had the element of surprise, and there was no one to stand in their way. Taylor knew that was too much to hope for.

A broad ten metre column-like object that a second before was inanimate suddenly began to rotate and open in many angles. They could not work out what they were seeing for a moment, so nobody reacted. But as four legs expanded out from the body, they knew they were in trouble. Long arms slid out from the body, and light glistened off two metre-long gun barrels. Blades were slung under the entire length of the barrel, with barbs at the muzzle end.

"Cover!" Taylor hollered.

Babacan opened fire with the Hydra, and several others

joined him as everyone went forward to find any protection they could. Taylor hit the side of one of the pods and peered out from around it as the huge monster opened fire. Its first shot recoiled violently and soared towards Babacan who was advancing slowly as he fired. The shot hit the Hydra and blew in a spectacular and horrifying burst of light. The gun was blown apart, and Babacan was thrown five metres back. He rolled and tumbled, smashed into one of the pods, and went limp. Taylor had to hope he survived, but in the meantime, he forced himself to go back to the problem.

He took aim at the head of the creature. It was not hard to hit for it was a metre and a half wide. He fired three carefully aimed shots, but they did nothing. Then it turned its other weapon towards him and fired. He leapt back as the shot impacted, and he felt shreds of the pulse splash over his armour and could smell it melting the alloy. He quickly got up and ran to the next pod where Jones was dug in and firing a few shots.

"Got any great ideas?" Jones asked as he ducked down beside him.

Taylor looked out for the creature once more. It was now bearing down on their start position where Wilcox was lifting the AT gun onto its mount. Taylor saw the creature begin to take aim at the weapon, and he knew he had to act; it might be their only chance.

"Hey, asshole!" he shouted and ran out from cover. He fired his rifle repeatedly at the creature. Every single shot bounced from its hard shell armour until finally his magazine was empty, but the creature turned one of its cannons around to fire on him.

"Shit!"

He threw down his rifle and ran as fast as he could. A pulse smashed into the ground behind him, and more shrapnel of energy rushed past his head. A second shot landed even closer, but he was relieved to hear the thunderous crack of the AT gun, and the crunching sound it made finding a target. It sounded like a skull being caved in.

Taylor stopped and turned around. The monster had stopped chasing him and frozen for a moment. There was an almost half-metre exit wound in the front of its torso where the shell had gone clean through. Taylor waited and hoped for it to collapse, but it appeared more stunned than anything.

"Hit it again!" Jones bellowed.

But even as he said, it the monster spun around and charged towards Wilcox at a remarkable pace. The rest of the unit were laying down fire as it charged, but there seemed no stopping it. Wilcox stayed at his gun until the very last and managed to squeeze off one more shot as it bore down on him. The shell hit the creature's torso just a metre below the previous shot, once again bursting through its body, but there was no stopping it this time.

The beast raised one of its weapons and cut down with the blade on the huge barrel. The barb struck Wilcox's helmet and split his body all the way down to his abdomen; the blade sliced the AT gun in half all in one. It was a horrific sight, but all Taylor could think was, how the hell could they take it down? He pulled out his Assegai and flicked it into position, but the prospect of going anywhere near the creature in hand-to-hand was terrifying.

"What do we do, Taylor?" Jones asked.

They watched the entire unit continue laying down

fire, but the creature turned back to them and opened fire indiscriminately with both cannons. Pulses of light smashed into the floor and walls all around them, and many hunkered down for cover in the hope they wouldn't be seen.

Taylor looked around for some answer, but it was Alita that his eyes found. She was hunkered down in cover, clutching her carbine. She was frozen solid, and her face was pale. She stared out in front of her and was unable to even turn her head. She was in shock. It pushed Taylor over the edge. He got up with nothing but his Assegai and shield in hand. Jones' hand grabbed at him.

"What are you doing? You can't fight that in single combat!"

Taylor looked down at the Assegai and back at the creature. It was constantly turning and shooting at targets as his people went from cover to cover. Then he noticed the huge holes that Wilcox had punched in its body with the AT gun. He retracted his Assegai and holstered it. Jones was relieved, but what Taylor did next was the last thing he expected. He drew out a grenade from his armour and ran towards the creature without any fear at all.

"Taylor!" Jones screamed, but it was too late.

The Lieutenant lifted his rifle to lay down covering fire, although he knew it would do little more than to be a distraction.

Taylor rushed at the creature and ducked under one of its legs. It swung for him with a blade, but he turned and spun, punching off the side of the barrel as it went past. He then jumped as high as he could, primed the grenade, and launched it inside the lower entry wound on the creature. As he landed, he was struck by the barrel from the return swing and launched ten metres. He smashed into a group of pods, one bursting in half as he passed through it. A red viscous-like jelly burst over him as he hit the second pod and dropped heavily to the floor.

"Cover!" Jones ordered.

They ducked down and prayed as the grenade rang out. Compressed inside the creature's torso, the explosion was massive and echoed from the ceiling. Fragments of metal, blood, and tissue were launched in every direction. A half-metre length of the creature's armour smashed into the pod beside Jones and pierced deeply. He knew it would have killed him outright if it had been a little closer.

Jones slowly got up and looked around at the carnage. He wasn't sure what part of the creature was organic and what was machine, as it was scattered in equal measure.

"Everyone okay?"

But they were too horrified to answer. Jones saw Taylor lying lifelessly in a pool of the disgusting red fluid. He rushed to the Colonel's side and turned him over. As he did so, he heard a groan and breathed out in relief at finding him alive.

"You're crazy, you know that, right?"

Taylor groaned again and wiped the liquid from his face and brushed it off his equipment.

"Yeah, and we're still alive."

Jones helped him to his feet. They looked over at Babacan being carried between two of the others. He could barely support his own weight, but he still looked up and nodded at Taylor in appreciation.

"Let the drones carry Babacan. We have work to do. We must keep moving. Longer this takes us, the more people we lose up there. If it takes too long, we won't get off this fucking place at all."

Taylor turned and carried on. He got up to a jogging pace and quickly felt pain shrieking through his body. He was limping slightly on his left leg, but he fought through the agony. He looked back to check on the bomb and could see the two carrying it were not far behind.

"How much further?"

"As far as we can take it, Jones."

Suddenly, a door opened, and six Morohta warriors rushed out towards them. Taylor turned, deflected a shot with his shield, and ran right at the first one. He smashed it off its feet, and with his shield held high drove his Assegai deep. Gunfire rang out as the others with it were cut down. He pulled out the Assegai to strike again, but the wounded creature swung the stock of its weapon towards him. The sharp edges cut into his jaw and up to his lip, but he quickly countered. He lifted up the Assegai and plunged it down into the warrior's neck until it went limp and collapsed.

"Keep moving!" he shouted, getting up to pace once again and ignoring the blood pouring down his neck. They carried on for another hundred metres when the chasm opened up into a vast underground canyon lake. It spanned out as far as the eye could see, and even the mouth was several hundred metres wide. A hundred metres into the water along a metal walkway was a green illuminated tower. It reached up to the ceiling and into a vertical corridor that seemed to rise to the surface.

"This is it, this is what Irala meant," said Jones.

Taylor looked around suspiciously for any sign of danger, but there was nothing. For a moment he marvelled at the beauty of what they were beholding. It was a magical sight, and Jones was clearly thinking the same.

"Be a damn tragedy to destroy this level of beauty," said Jones.

"Not as much as it would be to see Earth die."

Taylor pointed to the two carrying the weapon.

"You two, Jones, Antos, on me. The rest of you hold your ground, and do not let anything pass!"

He led the way forward to the gantry over the water that led to the tower. It was just two metres wide and made of a widely dispersed mesh that allowed you to see every glimmer of movement of the water below. He ran faster and faster towards the tower. Every pace he drew nearer, he expected some new danger to step out from the far side, and yet nothing came. They reached the end; the gantry circled around the tower and was a complete dead end. The base of the tower was ten metres thick and glowed from many semi-transparent windows.

Engravings and rune-like letters were cut and painted over almost every piece of surface area, but it meant nothing to any of them. Taylor placed his hand on the side of the structure and could feel the warmth it was transmitting. He could also feel a pulsating that was not unlike a heartbeat.

"What is it, machine, living, or what?"

Taylor shrugged. "Soon enough it will be nothing at all."

He gestured for the weapon to be placed down on the far side of the gantry where it could not be seen from where they had entered. Taylor and Jones took up positions either side of the spherical bomb, just as they had practiced.

"Are you ready for this?"

Jones nodded.

"They each placed a hand on the exact points they had been taught, twisting their hands back and forth to points as if they were opening a safe. They finally heard a clicking sound, and the space beneath their hands slid open to reveal a small keypad. The language was Krys, but it didn't matter; they had memorised the sequence.

Jones looked back into Taylor's eyes one last time, but Taylor did not hesitate.

"Three, two, one..." he said.

He punched the eight-digit code in just as Jones did in exact sequence. The keypad flashed three times and displayed a countdown.

"That's it, no going back," said Jones.

"Let's get the fuck out of this damned place."

They rushed back along the gantry and could already hear gunfire as they approached the rest of the team. But it was nothing more than a light skirmish.

"They really screwed up in defending this place."

"Yes, a mistake they are not likely to make twice. So let's be sure to make the best of this while we can," Taylor replied.

They reached the line of Immortals. They were finishing off a Stalker with sustained fire until it finally dropped dead.

"Time to go on home!" Taylor shouted to them all.

They got to their feet and got to a running pace. They passed over the trail of bodies they had left in their wake when they reached the body of Wilcox. It was being recovered by two of the drones. The two halves of his upper body flopped about as internal organs fell to the floor. It was a sickening sight, but they had no time to handle it in any better manner. They rushed to the elevator floor, and Taylor pointed for Babacan to do whatever he had to in order to activate it. He obliged, and they heard it power up and begin to move. They were almost clear and in the shaft when the chameleon-like armoured creature stepped into view. It reached in, and grabbed Jones by his right leg and pulled.

The Lieutenant was launched off his feet. His head smashed into the floor of the elevator, and he was dragged forward. Taylor jumped forwards to reach for his hand, but it wasn't quick enough. Jones flew out of the narrowing gap to the elevator shaft, and a second later they were rising up at rapid speed and could do nothing.

"Stop, go back down!" Taylor cried.

Babacan tried to manipulate the controller once again, but he could do nothing, and they continued up to the surface. Taylor had not felt so powerless in a long time, and he felt his blood boil with rage.

"He can't survive against that thing," said Bailey, but Taylor didn't want to hear it.

"Yes, he can. We are not leaving him behind!"

* * *

Jones was launched from the elevator until he felt the alien's grip release. He landed hard on the floor and rolled to a halt. He was back on his feet quickly and reached down for his rifle, only to find it had been yanked free when he was torn from the elevator. His hand reached for his Assegai, and he activated it and his shield, taking up a guard position and preparing to defend himself. The alien just stood in front of him as if with no fear or concern at all. Jones was utterly terrified but did everything he could to hide it.

"You should never have stepped foot on this sacred ground," said the creature.

"Yeah, well maybe you shouldn't have come looking for trouble."

"How can you ever believe you can win? You are small and weak. You are a toy to be played with until we grow tired of doing so."

"Then you know nothing about the Human race."

"You do not know who I am, do you?"

"Should I?"

"Prince Ganbaatar, son of Bolormaa, the Undefeated Scourge."

Jones tried to imagine what Taylor would say, and to feel the courage that he would.

"Undefeated? There is always a first time for everything. You are no Prince of mine. I am William Jones of the Immortals, and you will remember that name until the moment I drive this blade through your skull."

"Immortals?" Ganbaatar asked.

He began to laugh in a slow and echoey way that resonated through the chasm.

"It will be my pleasure to not just kill you, but all of these Immortals. Nothing can stand in our way."

"Indeed, well I am."

The alien didn't respond. He only stretched out his arms and opened his hands palm forward. Jones couldn't work out what he was doing, when suddenly a blade launched from each of the insides of his arms and he grasped them at the hilt. Each blade was a metre and a half long and straight. They glistened like diamonds under light, despite the dimly lit environment. Jones could see the alien was enjoying himself, and his sense of confidence was overpowering.

"Why do you want to end our lives? To what end? What do you get out of it?"

But Ganbaatar said nothing and began circling him. Then he roared with anger and rushed forward with both blades in a quick cut towards Jones' head.

* * *

The Immortals rushed off of the ramp of the elevator but stopped as they realised Taylor was still aboard.

"What are you doing?" Alita pleaded.

"I will not leave him behind."

"But you'll die," she replied, tears seeping down her face.

Taylor's comms unit flashed, and he accepted to hear Cohen's voice.

"Taylor, come in."

"I'm here," he replied solemnly.

"Have you accomplished your mission?"

"Yes."

"Then get back up here. We can't hold on much longer!"

"Lieutenant Jones is stuck down there, dragged back down by that monster I thought you killed. I'm going in after him."

"Taylor, that is the spawn of Bolormaa," Jafar added.

"I don't care. I left a Jones to the enemy once before. I won't do it again!"

"Taylor you..." began Cohen.

But Taylor cut the signal off.

"They are your responsibility now, Lieutenant," he said to Alita, "You get them to safety."

She couldn't find any more words to say to try and stop him, and he put his hand into the console and activated the elevator. As it began to move, he pulled the huge Morohta hammer from his back and held it in readiness in both hands. He soon vanished from Alita's view. He was trying to psych himself up mentally as he felt his grip clench tighter on the hammer.

"Come on, Jones, you can make it," he said quietly as the elevator increased in pace.

* * *

Jones' head smashed into one of the skeletal-like support beams, and he felt the impact ring through his ears, knowing it was only his helmet that kept him conscious, let alone alive.

He looked back just in time to see Ganbaatar's blade coming for him once again. He raised up his shield again, and the impact smashed him out and away from the wall. His legs were weak now, and his right arm was bleeding badly from a deep cut below the shoulder. Ganbaatar paced confidently around him as if toying with him. Jones knew he was no match for the creature, but he was determined to land a strike. He acted even more exhausted and weak than he was, and as Ganbaatar rushed forward again with a vertical cut, he began to step one way to counter and then immediately leapt the other, coming up on the inside of the beast's right arm. He thrust his Assegai into the centre of the arm, and Ganbaatar let out a shriek of agony.

Jones smiled, realising the alien's arrogance had allowed

him to land a strike he should never have been able to make. The sword fell from its wounded arm, but a moment later the open hand lashed out at his head. It hit like a freight train and threw him back off his feet. As he rolled and tumbled, he finally came to a standstill as he smashed into a metal rail. He felt his Assegai drop from his hands. He could hear it bounce and fall, and to his horror the railing was all that had stopped him from falling down a deep canyon and into the blackness.

His weapon was gone now, and with it all hope of hurting the alien Prince. Taylor's words of close combat rang through his head now, as he understood how true they were. Ganbaatar seemed to patch over the wound with something from his suit that burnt into his flesh and caused him to screech once again. It was a dreadful sound that emanated in Jones' ears. He knew he was finished now and made no attempt to fight back. He got up onto one knee and smiled at the creature.

"If I can make you bleed, many more will follow in my stead."

The creature paced slowly towards him as if savouring every moment before the kill. It was clear from the look on its face that it was in pain, and that pleased Jones. It stopped as it loomed over him and raised its sword in the air to take his head.

"You are not an Immortal!" it said bitterly.

"That's where you're wrong!" a voice roared beside them.

Out of the dark, Taylor swung the hammer before the creature could react and hit it square in the chest with all the force he could muster, as if he were trying to fell a tree. There was a flash as the explosive charge ignited, and the combined power of the strike and the charge smashed Ganbaatar over the railings. Jones watched speechless as he tumbled over the edge, shrieking as he fell into darkness and out of view. He turned back to Taylor and shook his head.

"Why did you come back for me?"

"Because I'd like to think that you would do the same for me."

Taylor grabbed his arm and hauled him to his feet.

"Have we still got time to make it?" Jones asked breathlessly as they ran towards the elevator.

"We can only try."

They leapt into the elevator, and Taylor quickly hit the control to get them moving, but he did not relax yet. He held his hammer in two hands at the entrance and waited for the first sign of movement. He half expected to be attacked once again as they had done before, but to his relief, they lifted up above the opening and began soaring to the surface.

CHAPTER THIRTEEN

"We have to leave now. We cannot wait for Taylor any longer!" Nichols shouted.

Jafar said nothing, for he didn't want to condemn his friend.

"He knew the risks of this mission like everyone else. If he has placed the device, then the mission is a success, and we should leave while we still can!"

Jafar looked to Cohen to see she was nodding in agreement. He then looked to Irala, whose projection was still before them. The bridge lit up with a flash as one of the Aranui vessels erupted on screen.

"Do we go? Do we leave the man who got us this far?" Jafar asked them all.

"He of all people would never have us sacrifice all our lives in some vain attempt at rescue," replied Irala.

Jafar was about to make the call when Taylor came over the comms.

"We're on our way!" he shouted, "Don't go without us!"

Jafar signed with relief, and Cohen leapt in to assist.

"Get a fighter squadron down there to support them. Let's bring our people home!"

Taylor rushed out of the elevator with Jones at his side. There was no sign of life in sight, but they could hear the roar of engines overhead and saw a Sky King descending. Bailey and Antos were at the door, and Taylor could see Alita through the cockpit window.

"Come on!" Antos called out.

They leapt to a sprinting pace as gunfire hit the ground around them. Taylor looked up to see three Morohta warriors firing down on them, but they could do nothing except rush on and hope their shields would cover them. Antos leaned out of the side door and took aim at them, laying down fire from the cover of the craft. Finally, they reached the door and jumped inside. They quickly lifted off the ground as Antos passed a rifle each to Taylor and Jones.

The Sky King rotated, bringing their attackers in full view, and they opened up with a volley of fire as they began to gain height. Two of the Morohta warriors were cut down until finally they accelerated beyond view and range. Antos hit the ramp door shut, and Jones slumped back in relief. Taylor went to the cockpit and slid into the co-pilot's seat.

"I told you to get out of here," he said to Alita.

"And do you always follow your orders to the letter, Colonel?" she asked coyly.

He reached across and laid a hand on her shoulder.

"Thank you," he said sincerely.

They soared up into the atmosphere as a fighter darted past them. He checked, and they had three minutes left.

He glanced back to Jones who could see what he was looking at.

"How long?"

"Three minutes."

Jones shook his head. "Does your luck never run out, Colonel?"

Taylor shrugged.

I sure hope not.

They soon broke atmosphere, and Taylor's smiled was quickly removed by the devastation they found. More than half the fleet was destroyed, and it looked like a graveyard of ships. There were many of the Morohta vessels as badly mauled as their own, but not in such number.

Alita ducked and weaved the ship around debris and gunfire as they made their final approach. Just as they were about to reach the docking bay entrance, they felt an impact hit their tail and knock them out of line with the bay entrance. The tail smashed into the frame and was cut clean off, as the rest of the craft tumbled through the opening and crashed into the docking bay floor. They kept spinning and sliding and felt a violent drop. The undercarriage was torn off, and they held on for their lives. They hit the far wall and came to a violent stop.

"Everyone okay?" Alita asked.

She had been the only one that was strapped in. The others had been tossed around the ship and lay scattered across the floor.

"Perfect," Taylor replied sarcastically.

He looked down at his counter. One minute and thirty seconds left.

"This is the Commander speaking. All vessels prepare to jump," said Cohen's voice over the comms.

"No!" Taylor yelled.

He tapped the console on his arm and got a direct feed to the bridge.

"Commander, we can't jump until we know they can't. We cannot afford their fleet following us back home!"

"If we wait any longer, we'll be dead, anyway, Colonel!"

"And if we don't it could all have been for nothing. If we take their fleet back to the Solar System, who will be left to stop it?"

They watched through the hole in their own ship as dozens of fighters made combat landings all around them. Many of them were as damaged as they were. Taylor got to his feet and stepped out with his hammer still in hand. He watched through one of the shielded fighter bay entrances so that he could have a view down to the planet like a window into space.

"Come on, you bastards," he said to himself.

Jones stepped up beside him to watch for the culmination of all their work. As he did, they both noticed a crippled Sky King trying to make her way to the landing bays. Hot on her tail was a Mech fighter relentlessly strafing her tail, but Taylor knew there was nothing he could do for them. But a second later one of the Guam's gun systems clipped the enemy ship, and the Sky King tumbled through into the landing bays, but the enemy craft continued on after her and rushed inside the Guam's bays. It hit the deck hard and slid to a halt.

The second it stopped moving a volley of gunfire erupted, and Taylor watched his unit lined up like a firing squad. They poured fire into the craft. The cockpit was riddled with fire, and he could see the pilot spasm as he was hit by multiple shots. A ramp on the side of the craft was blown off like some emergency release, and out poured ten Morohta warriors.

Taylor drew out his Assegai and tossed it to Jones. They all drew weapons and rushed at the enemy with shields forward as a wall. Taylor got to them first and smashed the front of the hammer into a creature, raising it over his head and crushing it with one explosive strike.

Jones hadn't slowed at all. He struck a creature with the edge of his shield and drove the Assegai deep into its chest, moving onto the next without any hesitation at all. It was then that Taylor stopped and watched in amazement as his new Immortals took the enemy apart. It brought back a flood of emotion for him, and he could only smile as he accepted he had found a new home and a new family. Antos got the last one with an Assegai thrust into the stomach, driving it vertically through the body, and tossing it to the ground in disgust.

As it came to an end, the bridge flashed with light, and they turned to the view down on the planet. Beams of light were bursting from holes in the surface, and the atmosphere was darkening as lightning-like flashes burst across the sky. The entire world began to dim as the skies were overcome with a thick black fog.

"So that is what it's like to destroy a world?" Jones asked.

Taylor shrugged. "New experience for me as well."

They were relieved to hear Cohen's voice come over the comms once again.

"All ships prepare to jump in five...four...three...two... one, jump!"

They stared at the crippled world as they rushed into the gateway. Many of the Morohta vessels were still shooting at them as they passed inside, and three of the frigates managed to enter the gateway with them. Just a few moments later, they burst back out of the gateway to where it had all begun - Ares 4. The enemy vessels fired a few more shots, but within ten seconds, the Ares defence grid joined the fray and bombarded their attackers. They were smashed by the sheer weight of fire.

All fell silent then. It was as if someone just flicked a switch. No more gunfire, explosions. No dogfights. Fires still burned on several of the vessels in the distance. Taylor was mesmerised by it all. He snapped out of it as he felt an arm wrap around his. He looked over to see that it was Alita. The red grime of his uniform smeared over her uniform as she nestled into him, but she didn't seem to care.

"This is the Commander speaking. Mission successful, welcome back home!"

Cheers rang out across the fighter bays where they stood, and Alita reached in and kissed Taylor. He could not resist turning and embracing her the same.

"We did it, you did it," she said as she leaned back in his arms.

"We shall overcome all adversity. We always do," he replied and kissed her once again. The triumphant feeling was overwhelming, and something he remembered well. This life was starting to feel so much more like his old one that he found his mind was being put at ease, even if his memories could not be.

"So what now?" she asked.

"It's not over, but it sure is a time to celebrate."

* * *

Taylor strode into the conference room of the Ares 4 colony as he had done before. He still wore the filthy and bloody uniform he had fought in, and Jones and Jafar were at his back. As they stepped inside, President Isaacs began to clap, and he was soon joined by every representative and official inside. But it was when Taylor noticed the empty seats of the Cholan people that he felt a raging anger inside. The round of applause seemed to go on for several minutes when Isaacs finally lifted his hand to call for silence and went on.

"Colonel Taylor, let me be the first to thank you on behalf of the Alliance of nations. I will be the first to admit I had my doubts that you had any place in our society today, but I was wrong. And I am glad to say I was wrong. Your achievements here have been truly beyond amazement, and we all thank you."

He fell silent as if expecting Taylor to provide some response.

"Will you now prepare for war?"

The tone in the room changed completely.

"Colonel, is this not a time to celebrate?"

"For the survivors of this battle, because they earned it, yes. For the rest of the Alliance, there is no time to rest. There is no room for error, no space for weakness or indecision. From tomorrow, until the day we see the Morohta again, there must not be a day when the shipyards are not building, the factories not running, and the recruits not training. We didn't win the war today. We barely won the battle. What we did win was an opportunity. An opportunity that if squandered we will likely never have again."

Isaacs was stunned for a moment, for it seemed the last response he expected to get.

"Do you really believe things are that dire, Colonel?"

"I know they are. Ask anyone who went to Khar Els, or rather anyone that lived to tell the tale. They are more powerful than any other race, and at a time when we are not prepared for war. Things need to change, and I intend to make sure they do. I don't know if you are a wartime leader or not, Mr President, but every change that is necessary to prepare us for this battle must be undertaken. Councillor Irala believes we might have won ourselves a year at the very most. That is not long to make the changes that will be necessary."

"And you agree with this analysis of our situation, Lord Jafar?"

"I do, and I intend to rally the independent factions of the Krys people before that time comes. Together we may be strong, but alone and separated, we cannot win this."

Isaacs looked downtrodden and depressed as he slumped back down in his seat. It was clearly not the celebrations and news he had been hoping for.

"Break this news however you want," added Taylor, "Tell the colonies of our success and let people celebrate it, but do not tell them we have won anything. The people need to know the seriousness of this situation. They have to know what they must do, and what is expected of them if they are to survive."

"You are talking conscription now? Your work and efforts have been greatly appreciated, Colonel, but that goes against our entire culture. Do you know the last time anyone was conscripted to fight?"

"Time to change, then, Mr President. Now, if you don't mind, we have dead to mourn, wounded to care for, and comrades to celebrate with; because the people that went with me to Khar Els, they earned it."

"Colonel Taylor, we have already arranged a grand banquet in honour of all those who undertook this mission. This is our way of saying thank you and supporting all those who sacrificed so much. At 1500 hours there will be a conference and remembrance for all those that were sadly lost, and a celebration will follow the likes of which you have never seen."

Fucking great!

"Will that be all?"

"Yes, thank you, Colonel. And do not forget how much we appreciate all your efforts."

Taylor turned and left with Jones and Jafar.

"Still making friends, I see?" Jones commented sarcastically.

"He's a fool," Taylor replied, shaking his head, "A few weeks will go by with some half hearted publicity stunt, and they we'll be right back where we are."

"I will not let that happen."

"No, Jafar? And how much say do you have on the Human element of this Alliance?"

Jafar said nothing.

"That's what I thought. All the fighting I do in my life, and I can't escape the politics. It is endless."

"You say that," added Jones, "But you have always meddled in politics, more than any person I can think that I have ever known or studied. For a fighting man, you surely do get involved in places your job never should."

"Yep, well sometimes, someone has to."

"Will!" a voice yelled.

They turned to see Cynara rushing towards Jones. She leapt into his arms. It brought a smile to his face as he thought back to Coco and Charlie. But as he was busy reminiscing, he felt a hand on his shoulder and pull him around. He turned and felt Alita's lips lock with his. He instantly felt his troubles and fears melt away. It was a relief. She leaned back in his arms once again.

"So what great medal is the President going to bestow on you this time?"

He shook his head. "Hopefully nothing."

"Taylor, this is Cynara, my wife. Cynara, this is Colonel Mitch Taylor."

"I know who he is. How could I not? He is practically family."

Taylor nodded in humble appreciation, many memories stirring in his mind.

"Without Taylor, I would never have come back alive. When I was all alone and lost, I had nowhere to turn and no way out. It was Taylor who came for me."

"Then I can never thank you enough. How can I ever begin to?"

"Honestly? You can get me a beer."

She smiled and then began to laugh.

"I can surely do that."

"Right now," he stated.

She wasn't sure how to take it, but he wasn't joking.

* * *

Taylor strode into the bar they had drunk at since arriving

at the station. Cheers rang out as they entered, despite the fact he still wore his filthy uniform and armoured suit. He didn't care to take it off, as it felt like home now. He stepped up the bar, and Cyn tried to get a drink for him, but she couldn't even get served. A glass was placed before Taylor and the bottle with it.

He ignored the glass and took the bottle, grabbed the cap by his teeth, and ripped it out before spitting it out. He turned around to address the crowd that waited for him to say some words.

"I wasn't born in this time and life, and I never wanted it. But in my short time here, I have come to gain friends and family that mean as much to me as those I once fought with in my first lifetime. When I awoke in this new life, I thought the whole world had gone crazy. But here we are. I want you to raise your glasses and drink to our victory, our fight, to all those we have lost, and for all the hard times to come. I salute you!"

He raised the bottle in salute and finally knocked it back in celebration.

* * *

It was not long until the President's speech now, and Taylor at last climbed into a shower. His head was soft from drink, but it at least served to numb the pain he felt. Blood and dirt flowed from his body, and he started to feel refreshed. He was beginning to appreciate now that he truly had been resurrected. He didn't feel out of place anymore because he now felt that perhaps he was destined to be here in this time and place, just as he had in his previous life.

He stepped out, pulled on a fresh uniform, and made his way to the door. As it opened, he found Jones leaning against the wall, waiting for him. A huge grin was stretched across his face.

"What?" Taylor asked suspiciously.

"I'm just thinking how you came back for me. The great Mitch Taylor risked everything, for me?"

Taylor stepped back and put his hands up before him.

"You're not gonna try and kiss me now, are you?"

Jones laughed. "Do you really believe I would have done the same for you?"

Taylor nodded.

"I want to believe so, because we Immortals, we are family. We have a bond that cannot be broken, not even in death. The day will come when our roles are reversed, and it may come sooner than you think."

"Then I hope and only pray I can rise to that occasion."

"Don't pray for it. Know it. There are too many uncertainties in life for you to worry. Now come on, let's see how much of a mess Isaacs can make of this."

They carried onwards and were soon joined by the rest of the Immortals. Taylor noted that every one of them walked taller and prouder now than they had ever done, and he was proud of them for it. They reached a ceremony hall and found it packed out with thousands of guests.

"This way, Colonel," said one of the ushers.

"Wherever I go, they go," he replied.

"As you wish, Sir."

They were led down the central corridor, passing line after line of serving personnel, reporters, and civilians of Krys, Aranui and Humans. Many clapped as they went by. When they reached the very front of the room, they were ushered into the front row a few metres in front of the podium.

"I never cared for all this pomp and ceremony," Taylor said to Jones.

"But you have to let them have it. Look at them. They need it."

Taylor reluctantly agreed with him. "Whatever gets the job done."

As he looked around, his eyes suddenly connected with Alita's. She was standing the other side of Jones with a broad smile. Her eyes were sparkling, and her entire body positively glowed. All Taylor could now think was that he could not afford to lose another one like her.

A few moments later a representative of the President stepped up to the podium to get things started. She was a beautiful young woman in a gleaming silver dress suit. She was short and of Asian descent. Taylor expected some big speech from her to frame the President's arrival, but her opening was short and to the point.

"Ladies and Gentlemen of the Alliance, I give you President Isaacs."

She stepped aside as he stepped up to take her position. He wore a pin sharp suit, and the worried wrinkles of his face were gone now through carefully and professionally applied make up. He looked confident and content, but did not smile.

"People of the Alliance!" he began.

His voice carried through speakers throughout the entire room, and screens above them displayed his address to the whole of the Solar System. Cameras floated around the room, filming from every angle.

"Just a few short days ago we were struck by tragedy

and adversity, the likes of which we could never have imagined."

Should have prepared for anything then, shouldn't you?

But he felt a nudge from Jones and realised he had actually spoken the words out, too. Jones was both smiling and appalled all at once, as a camera had been watching them, but the President didn't seem to have heard or noticed as he continued.

"Through this adversity, we as the Alliance have triumphed. It is through the hard work, effort, and sacrifice of so many that we have gotten through this horrific experience, but none more so than one man; a man who seemingly doesn't belong in this timeline, and yet came back to us in our greatest time of need. That man is Colonel Mitch Taylor. A hero among the Human race, and today he lives as a hero of the Alliance and an inspiration to us all!"

Roars of excitement and cheers rang out as people began to clap. For a full minute the President was drowned out and forced to wait for the noise to die down, although Taylor had no reaction at all. The President's words earlier had stuck with him, and all he saw was a man pandering to a crowd. He feared for what Isaacs would do now he could get away with a short-lived peace. The President looked down at him and smiled, but it seemed entirely false.

"But through all of the great achievements of Colonel Taylor, his Immortals, and all those who fought that battle together, let us now remember those who paid the ultimate sacrifice so that we may be here today. Our society has not known the scourge of war in most of our lifetimes, but I suspect the pain and suffering of loss remains a constant, no matter the time or place. Let us thank and remember all those we have lost in this battle, for they must never be forgotten."

Taylor started to blank out what the President was saying. His mind began to wander, but not to the sad losses he had endured now. It was Alita he pictured. He was daydreaming and oblivious to all that was around him. Several minutes passed when he was awoken by clapping and cheers from the crowd.

"As a final word, may I now call for a minute's silence so that we may reflect and remember all those who gave their lives?"

The room fell silent as everybody lowered their heads. Taylor tilted his head just slightly so that he could look past Jones and see Alita smiling back at him. The minute's silence seemed to go on forever but was broken by an alarm that rang out through the entire station. Taylor felt his heart sink at the thought of what might have caused it. A Navy officer rushed to the President's side and whispered in his ear. Then several of the high-ranking officers behind Isaacs poured out of the room through an exit at the back of the podium.

"What the hell is going on?" Jones asked.

Everyone waited for a word from the President.

"Can all personnel remain calm and report for duty immediately. That will be all," he said and quickly stepped down.

"This can't be good," Taylor muttered.

He rushed up to the podium to follow Cohen and the other Naval officers. Jones was close behind him and security did not question it. As he got to the door, Taylor looked back to his people.

"Gear up, and be ready for anything!" he ordered before

passing through the doorway.

"Where are they all going?" Jones asked breathlessly.

"To wherever this place is run from."

It took just over a minute to reach the bridge of the station. Taylor paced right up to Cohen and asked, "What the fuck is happening?"

But the Commander seemed unable to answer and stared at the screens. In the distance ahead they could see the remnants of the fleet they had brought back from Khar Els. Much of it was already under repair, though many of the vessels would be better off going to scrap. The gateway in the distance was opening, and everyone appeared to be waiting to see what was going to come through.

"Expecting trouble, Commander?"

"Someone has opened a gateway from Cholan space. We've got nothing out there."

"What do you think it is?"

Cohen shrugged, as she had no better idea than anyone else in the room. A single Cholan vessel had already come through the gateway and was stationary between the gateway and the Allied fleet. It was a small vessel and appeared to be no threat at all. Taylor squinted and looked at the ship, trying to imagine what their intentions were.

"You think they want to negotiate?"

"Or scout us out before they hit us with everything they have got. Why would the gateway still be open otherwise, Jones?"

Jafar strode into the centre of the room.

"Hail that ship!" he ordered.

"We can't get a response, Sir," one of the officers replied.

"Shoot them. Take them down before they can get a signal out," said Taylor.

Many of the officers in the room looked at Taylor in disgust.

"The Cholans are our ally," replied Cohen.

"Were; the moment they left us to die all that changed. Shoot them down now and lock the gateway!" Taylor demanded.

Even Jafar was unsure.

"Trust me, this is not how your allies operate. Had they been interested in helping, they would have done so when we needed it most."

"And if you are wrong, and we fire on a peaceful ally, we could start a war that was never necessary," added Cohen.

Jafar looked to Taylor and then to the President. No one was certain of how to respond except for Taylor, and nobody wanted to accept the possibility that he might be right. But before anyone could say another word, a swathe of Cholan vessels poured through the gateway. At their centre was the Nakbe, and within a few short moments, there were almost seventy Cholan vessels bearing down on them.

"Maybe they have come to offer their assistance."

"You're dreaming, Commander," replied Taylor, shaking his head.

"We are being hailed!"

"Put them through!" Jafar said quickly.

Almost ten seconds passed as they waited, and it felt like an eternity.

"If the Cholans turn on us, we're in deep trouble."

"Like we weren't before, Jones," replied Taylor.

A projection appeared of Admiral Eme. The sight of

the alien angered Taylor, for he would never forgive him for turning his back on them all.

"Admiral Eme, what is the meaning of this show of strength? What are your intentions?" Jafar asked.

Eme seemed to be looking around in various directions as if studying all that he was seeing from the bridge of the Nakbe. The uncertainty was exhausting and nail biting, but then the Admiral spoke.

"I am here on behalf of the Cholan people. We suffered greatly at the hands of a foreign invasion force. The Alliance of races failed to protect us, despite treaties intended to do so. As a member of the Alliance, we worked to uphold values that others have failed to protect. We have been betrayed. We have had no choice but to surrender to the Morohta will and fight alongside those who will fight beside us. The President of the Alliance has one hour to offer unconditional terms of surrender to me, or we will fire upon you."

Taylor turned back to look at the President. He was frozen solid in panic and fear, and no one else could find an answer. Taylor strode across the room and hit the switch on the comms panel to end the transmission.

"What do we do?" President Isaacs asked. He was shaking with fear.

Taylor took a deep breath and answered confidently.

"The only thing we can."